SHEIKH'S BABY
OF REVENGE

SHEIKH'S BABY OF REVENGE

TARA PAMMI

MILLS & BOON

First published in Great Britain 2018
by Mills & Boon, an imprint of HarperCollins*Publishers*
1 London Bridge Street, London, SE1 9GF

Large Print edition 2018

© 2018 Harlequin Books S.A.

Special thanks and acknowledgement are given to Tara Pammi for her contribution to the Bound by the Desert King series.

ISBN: 978-0-263-07444-4

MIX
Paper from
responsible sources
FSC™ C007454

This book is produced from independently certified FSC™ paper to ensure responsible forest management. For more information visit www.harpercollins.co.uk/green.

Printed and bound in Great Britain
by CPI Group (UK) Ltd, Croydon, CR0 4YY

CHAPTER ONE

"I'M ADIR AL-ZABAH, Your Highness, Sheikh of the Dawab and Peshani tribes."

He had no respect for the old king, for a man who subjugated and forced a woman—a weaker being—to bend to his will.

But Adir added a half bow to his greeting. Savage though he might be in comparison to the royal siblings Princes Zufar and Malak and Princess Galila, he knew customs and traditions.

Adir Al-Zabah stared at King Tariq of Khalia, watching like a hawk that soared the vast expanse of his desert abode, waiting for a flicker of recognition in the sorrow-filled eyes.

It was sorrow he recognized, wretched and absolute—something he had spied in his own reflection since he had heard the news of Queen Namani's death.

The genuine quality of it shocked him—one

glimpse into King Tariq's eyes was enough to understand that he had loved his wife.

Any sympathy Adir might have felt died under the resentment festering in his veins. He himself had not even been granted the right to mourn her publicly, the opportunity to honor her with the last rites.

He'd been denied the chance to set eyes on her even once in his life.

His last blood connection, gone in the flicker of a sunset. There would be no more letters telling him he was cherished, reminding him of the place he had left unclaimed for so long.

He was finally, completely alone in the world.

And all because of this king.

While King Tariq stared back at him with confusion clouding his eyes, one of the princes moved forward, blocking the sight of the old king's bowed form, as if to shield the pitiful sight of his father from Adir's eyes.

"I'm Crown Prince Zufar. If you have come to pay your final respects to Queen Namani, to pledge your allegiance to King Tariq—" Zufar's words were filled with a resentment that mirrored Adir's own, making Adir frown "—then consider it acknowledged."

Adir gritted his teeth. "I am the ruling Sheikh of the Dawab and Peshani tribes. We're independent tribes, Your Highness." He injected every ounce of mockery he felt into that address. "I do not acknowledge your or your king's authority over our tribes. Our way of living knows no liege."

Something almost like admiration glinted in Prince Zufar's eyes. Gone in the blink of an eye, it left Adir to wonder if he had only imagined it. Was he that desperate for a familial connection?

"This is a private time of mourning for the royal family. If you're not here to pay your respects, why did you request an audience with my father?"

Having to go through this man who had everything Adir had been denied grated like the rub of sand on an open wound. "It is the king's company I requested. Not yours."

Satisfaction glinted in Zufar's eyes, satisfaction that he had the right to deny Adir this. Or anything he could ask for. "My father is…*swimming* in his grief over his queen's death."

His queen's death, not my mother's death, thought Adir. The crown prince's words were revealing.

There was no…grief in the prince's eyes for his mother's death, unlike in his father's. No tenderness when he spoke of her. "He has not been in his right mind for several…months now."

Adir tilted his head in the direction of Prince Malak and Princess Galila. He didn't want to feel pity, he didn't want to consider the fragility of their feelings so soon after their mother's death. And yet he found himself doing just that. "You would have me open a cupboard full of skeletons in front of your younger siblings?" he added silkily.

Zufar paled under his dark, olive skin. Not that his arrogance dimmed even a bit. "Threats will get you nowhere, Sheikh Adir."

"So be it. I'm your… I'm Queen Namani's son."

The statement he had repeated so many times to himself, in his own head, now reverberated in the chilling silence that ensued. A soft gasp emerged from the princess's mouth while Prince Malak scowled.

The antagonism in Zufar's eyes multiplied a thousand fold, roped with disbelief and a flash of fleeting pain.

Adir shifted his feet to gain a glimpse of King Tariq. His shoulders bowed, the old man stared at Adir searchingly. As if he could find a glimpse of his beloved wife, Adir realized with a frown. "Namani's son? But—"

"Do not deny it, Your Highness. The truth shines in your eyes."

Accusation painted every tense line of Zufar's body. "Father?"

But King Tariq couldn't shift his gaze from Adir. "You're Namani's son? The child she—"

"The newborn you banished to the vagaries of the desert, yes. The child you separated from its mother."

"You're our brother?" Princess Galila interjected. "But why—"

"Namani…she had an affair…" King Tariq stuttered.

"She fell in love with another man and was punished for it." Adir didn't pull his punches.

The king's face crumpled.

"And what is it that you want, on the eve of her death, Sheikh Adir?" Prince Zufar said coldly.

"I want what my mother wanted for me."

"How would you know what Queen Namani… what she wanted for you if you've never met her?" Princess Galila asked, her tone feather-soft.

"She was forced to give me up but she did not abandon me."

Prince Malak who had been calmly watching the proceedings until now moved to stand beside his father. "What do you mean, she did not abandon you?" A caustic laugh fell from his mouth. "What is it that the queen gave you that makes you talk of her as if you knew her?"

His gaze swept over the royal siblings and Adir frowned. He was missing something. They did not pounce to defend their mother's memory. No other interest showed on their faces except the shadow of fear about what he would ask.

"I did know her. Somehow, she found a way to keep in touch with me. She wrote me over the years, encouraged me to rise in the world. Told me how much she…cared for me. Told me what my place is in this world. It is proof enough," Adir replied, choosing his words with cutting precision. "Every year on my birthday, she wrote letters and made sure they reached me. Letters telling me who I was."

"She wrote to you? The queen?"

"By her own hand."

"What do you want, Sheikh Adir? Why are you here?"

Adir faced Prince Zufar, determination running in his veins. "I want the king's acknowledgment that I'm Queen Namani's son. I want the world to know that I'm royal-born. I want my rightful place in Khalia's lineage."

"No." Zufar's tone rang out before Adir had barely finished. "All it will cause is a scandal."

He glanced at his father's form, his faraway gaze. Despite himself, Adir felt a stirring of pity for the old king. It was clear that he mourned his queen with all his heart.

"My father will become a laughingstock of the entire country if your origins come out. She—"

He broke off. "I will not let her selfish actions scandalize our family now, even after she's gone. As if she hasn't caused us enough harm. If you're the great sheikh your tribes claim you to be, you'll understand that I have to put Khalia first. There is no place for you here, Sheikh Adir."

"I would like to hear it from the king."

"My decision *is* the king's decision. I will not bring scandal to our house by declaring to the world what my mother has done."

"And if I refuse to follow your dictates?"

"Be careful, Sheikh Adir. You're threatening the crown prince."

"Are you worried that I will want to rule Khalia, Prince Zufar? That I will ask for a slice of your immense fortune? Because if so, then let me tell you, I have no intention of taking anything from you. I have no use for your wealth. All I want is recognition."

"And you will not have it, not as long as I'm alive. You are nothing but my mother's dirty secret, a stain on our family."

The words came at Adir like invisible punches,

all the more lethal for the truth in them that he had always tried to fight.

He was her dirty secret, banished to the desert without a second thought. "Watch your words, Prince Zufar. They carry heavy consequences."

"Have you not wondered why she asked you to claim your right only after she was gone? Why she wrote to *you* but never confided in *us* that we have a brother?"

"She was protecting you and the reputation of the royal family. She was—"

"Queen Namani—" Prince Zufar's words came through gritted teeth "—was a selfish woman who thought of nothing and no one but herself. Writing to you, I am sure, was nothing more than indulging in childish sulking. Behaving without considering the consequences…to you, to her or to any of us. It was cruel to lure you here when she knew nothing could come of it."

"And if I spill the truth anyway?" Adir hated the bitterness in his tone, cringed inwardly at the fear in the king's eyes. For years, he had watched his mother's family from afar. His mother's words about how spoiled they were, how undeserving of all the respect and privilege that were their due, had festered in his blood. "If I tell the world anyway?"

"I will not react to your threats, Sheikh Adir. The shame, if you spill it, will be yours and hers alone. Not ours. Leave now. Or I will have the guards throw you out as if you were nothing but a vulture circling at a time of mourning. If you had been anything but her bastard, you would have had better taste than to threaten my father at such a time of grief."

In the flickering shadows of the darkness, punctured only by gaslights flickering here and there, the view from the window out of which she meant to jump looked like absolute nothingness to Amira Ghalib.

Emptiness with no relief in sight. An abyss with no bottom.

Like her life had been for the past twenty-six years. Like the prospect of marrying Prince Zufar, like her future as Queen of Khalia.

She snorted and smiled into the darkness.

Ya Allah, she was getting morbidly morose. But

then that was what five days of being her father's prisoner and a punch to the jaw had done to her.

Of pretending to her friend Galila that she had been clumsy again, that she had walked straight into a pillar. Of once again being the object of indifference to her betrothed. Of being nothing but a means to an end to her power-obsessed father.

She had even less freedom here at the palace of Khalia than her own home, and her house on the best day was a cage. Here, all eyes were on her.

But future queen or not, she needed escape. Just for a few hours.

Having failed to locate the flashlight she'd been looking for—her father's watchdog had probably confiscated it from her suite—Amira looked through the window again. She remembered that there was a short ledge there, a rect-angular protrusion to cover the window on the lower floor. Big enough for her to land on with both feet.

From there, it would be another sideways jump to the next ledge.

From there, another jump onto the curved stairway on the other side, the stairway that was un-used even by servants and staff. And she would be free of the guard outside her suite, free of her father and free of her obligations.

She could walk to the stables, bribe the teenage boy there and go for a ride on the mare she had befriended the other day. She could just wander down the exquisitely manicured gardens the late Queen Namani had famously tended herself.

For a few hours, she could do whatever she wanted.

There is a ledge there, she repeated to herself.

All she had to do was hold her breath and jump.

Heart pounding, she climbed over the win-dowsill. Her legs dangled as she peered into the darkness, letting her eyes and ears adjust to the sounds and sights of the night. A horse's whinny, the soft tinkle of water from the famed fountain in courtyard, the tap-tap of soles on the tiled walkway reached her ears.

Night-blooming jasmine filled her nostrils.

Already, she felt calmer. It was a lovely night to escape.

She smiled and jumped.

* * *

"You could have killed yourself. At best. At worst, broken all the bones in your body."

Any breath that might have been left in her lungs after she'd landed wonkily on her knees whooshed out of Amira's lungs.

She froze, the low, gravelly voice from the dark corner of the stairway sending shivers down her spine. Fear and something else swamped her. She blinked and peered through the quiet to see a shadowy outline.

Catlike eyes, amber-hued, stared back at her. Moonlight came in patches through the archway, outlining the man. He was blurry because she had forgotten her glasses.

But she could still make out broad shoulders that tapered to lean hips and powerful thighs. She searched for his face. Square jaw, sharp blade of a nose, high forehead.

Her gaze went back to his eyes. Eyes that were staring at her with unhidden curiosity.

Was he a royal guard? Another spy her obsessed father had set on her? Or worse, a guest of the palace?

No, anything would be better than her father's spy. She would even prefer to brave her betrothed and explain herself than to face her father.

And if it was her father's spy...

As if even her flesh remembered, a shaft of pain pulsed up her jawline and she flinched.

She could swear his scowl deepened the darkness as the man emerged from the shadows. "Are you hurt?"

"No. I'm…fine." She dusted her palms on her thighs and winced. The skin of her palms had been pierced when she had tried to break her fall with them.

"You're not a natural liar, *ya habibiti.*"

The upper-class aristocratic accent—similar yet different from her own or from the prince's—caught her interest. With his perfect diction and the natural command in his very stillness, he could be a visiting royal—the last person she needed to be seen with. Or to have recognize her, come tomorrow.

He took another step toward her.

Still on her knees, Amira scooted back. Pains

and aches forgotten, all she wanted was to get away from the…interesting stranger.

Whether he noticed her retreat or not, his long strides continued to eat up the distance between them. "Let me see if you're hurt. You landed so hard you could have broken something."

Another scoot back. At this rate, her knees were going to get skinned. "I did not…break anything."

"Let me be the judge of that."

Her normally placid temper simmered. "Since I have a degree in nursing, I think I can judge whether I broke something or not." She hissed a breath out. "Please…just leave. I'll be on my way in a couple of minutes."

"You don't have to fear me."

She was panicked, yes, but strangely, there was no fear in it.

She took a deep breath. Sandalwood, combined with something utterly masculine, filled her lungs as he reached her, settling into a strange tightness in her lower belly.

Arrested by her body's reaction—neither flight

nor fight but more of a languid uncoiling low in her belly—she looked up at him.

Straight white teeth flashed at her when he smiled. "You intend to stay there?"

She nodded, aware of how stupid she must look, mooning over him and yet unable to stop.

"I'm perfectly fine with having a conversation on the...dirty floor," he said matter-of-factly. And before she could comprehend, he sank down on his knees with a fluid grace that was reminiscent of a jungle predator.

The traveling moon chose that exact moment to cast a bright, silvery glow through the archway, illuminating the planes of his face.

Breath arrested, Amira stared.

Deep-set amber eyes glinted with humor, and even that couldn't stop her appraisal. As if hand-chiseled by a master sculptor, he was breathtakingly handsome.

There was almost something royal about those features, something familiar yet painfully elusive.

She could see a high forehead, the sharp blade of a nose, weather-beaten skin that glinted dark gold—which told her he spent quite a lot of time in the harsh sun—and a defined jawline that invited her fingers' touch. Breathing shallowly, she fisted her hands in the folds of her gown.

His lashes flicked down to where she hid her hands and then up, that glimmer of humor deepening in his eyes.

"Tilt your head forward so that I may better look at you," he said in a low voice, no less commanding for its softness.

Years of obedience browbeaten into her, Amira dutifully did. Only when his gaze moved over every inch of her face with a penetrating intensity did she realize what she had done.

Color filled her cheeks. Instead of moving back, instead of lowering her eyes as she had been taught again and again by her father, she used the moment to study him some more.

A sharp hiss from his mouth jerked her gaze to his. In the flash of a breath, the humor disappeared, replaced by a dark vein of anger. His amber eyes glowed.

He lifted his hand to her face and Amira instantly cringed back. The softening of his expression told her what she had done. Shame filling her, she looked down at her palms. Hard concrete at her knees pulled her back to reality.

It was high time she was on her way. He was tying her insides into strange knots.

"May I touch you?"

His husky question jerked her gaze to his face again.

She thought she saw him swallow and that was strange.

"I promise I mean you no harm."

His eyes were deep pools, devoid of the barest expression, and yet there was an intrinsic trust deep in her belly that he would keep his word. That this was a man who didn't raise his hands against the weaker sex or people dependent on his mercies, for any reason. Not the least of which would be to establish his own superiority or to enforce his will.

Yet power seemed to emanate from his very pores. He would command any room he entered. And as to his will—she would bet any man or woman would surrender to it easily. With plea-sure, in the latter case.

Slowly, she nodded. Something in her leaped quietly—anticipation, she realized. With every cell in her being, she wanted to feel this man's touch, however fleetingly.

She thought he would pull her to her feet. Instead, his fingers landed on her jaw with such gentleness that hot tears prickled behind her eyelids.

"These are fingerprints marring your lovely cheek." The words were devoid of emotion, feeling. Contained violence shimmered in his stillness. He was *furious* at the sight of the bruise on her jaw.

That simple concern on her behalf sent sorrow spiraling through her.

She closed her eyes, loathe to betray her weakness in front of him. She had never shed a single tear, even when her father's palm once landed on her jaw with such force that her head had jerked back, leaving her with neck pain for weeks. But now…she felt like stretched glass.

As she stoppered the emotion flowing through her, she felt other things. It was as if her senses were slowly opening up. His huge body gave out warmth on the chilly night, enveloping her like her childhood blanket—a reminder of her mother.

The scent of him—the more she breathed it, the more she wanted to—a tantalizing mixture of sandalwood and horse and pure man.

His fingers turned her jaw to the moonlight so that the bruise, which she hadn't covered after washing off her makeup, was visible. The pad of his thumb traced it and she flinched. More from the heat his touch generated than from pain.

A sharp curse flew from his mouth. "Forgive me, I promised not to cause you harm."

"You didn't," she said automatically.

He raised a brow. "No?"

"Our skin has thousands and thousands of nerve centers that react to external stimuli, did you know? Your palm is rough against my skin and also, I'm barely ever touched by anyone other than my father—and not in such a leisurely, soft way, either—so I feel a flash burn where your skin touches mine—" when his brows rose, she hurried to explain "—not like fire burns us, more pleasurable than that, and I believe that's why I flinched. Because even pleasure, especially when it's unexpected and unfamiliar to the recipient, causes flinching."

The utter silence that ensued sent blood pooling up her neck and into her cheekbones. She clamped her palms over her mouth. No wonder her father got aggravated whenever she opened her mouth.

A slow smile dawned in his eyes, causing lines at the ends of his eyes and adorable creases in his cheeks. His teeth flashed at her again and that smile made him a thousand times more gorgeous.

"I state facts and run my mouth endlessly when I'm anxious or agitated or upset or sad or angry. My father thinks I do it to ignore his dictates and to insult him."

"And when you're happy?"

She smiled. "You're very smart, aren't you? You know, people think intelligence is…" She cleared her throat and she blushed fiercely again. "I do it when I'm happy, too, yes. Pretty much all the time, now that you make me think about it."

His smile turned into laughter. It boomed out of him. Low, gravelly, utterly sensuous, but also a little rough and strange. As if he didn't do it much.

Amira wanted to roll around in that smile. She wanted to be the one who caused his serious face to smile and laugh again and again. She wanted to spend an eternity with this exciting stranger who made her feel safe. She wanted to…

"I have to leave."

He sobered up. And frowned. "So I can take your word that you're not hurt?" He flicked another glance at her jaw. "Other than your jaw?"

"I misjudged the distance between the last ledge and the stairs, but I'm not hurt."

He nodded. "And what is so irresistible that you took such a dangerous route…? What is your name?"

Zara, Humeira, Alisha, Farhat…

"You're thinking up fake names."

She blinked. Like a hawk, he watched with predatory intensity. And something else… Possessiveness, perhaps.

She swallowed. "I would get into trouble if word gets out that I escaped my room or that I was wandering the palace without guard or that

I spent all this time in the dark with a stranger...
a lot of trouble."

"No one will know," he said. "I will get you
back to your room unharmed and undiscovered."

And all the while he tempted her, he watched
her. As if he found her endlessly fascinating. "I
don't know if I can trust you," she said.

His fingers pushed back a strand of hair that
brushed her jaw. Featherlight and tender, his
touch knocked down the little sense remaining
in her skull. "I think you do trust me. Which is
why you have lingered here so long already. All
you need to do is take the final step, *ya habibiti.*
We're strangers passing a few moments together
in a long life."

Another rough-padded finger lifted her chin
until she was gazing into his eyes. His nostrils
flared, the set of his jaw resolute. "I would have
your real name."

If he had commanded her, Amira would have
prevailed. But beneath that request was a thread
of longing that resonated in her soul. What could
such a commanding man want that he was ever
denied?

He was harshly beautiful, like the rugged landscape of the desert, and yet he looked at her with such pure need.

The last of her good sense and diffidence melted. Innocent she might be when it came to men but she already felt like she knew him.

He wouldn't hurt her.

"Amira…my name is Amira."

Fire awakened in his eyes. They both knew she had given him more than just her name in that moment.

He tilted his head—a regal nod for granting him the privilege of her real name. Warmth filled her chest. "I'm Adir."

"*Salaam-alaikum*, Adir."

"*Walaikum-as-salaam*, Amira."

He took her hand in his, completely engulfing hers. Sensations shimmered through her, flowing like a river from where their hands touched to spread all over her body. And then he was softly tugging her to him. Raising their clasped hands, he placed a soft kiss to the tender skin at her wrist.

It was a chaste kiss—nothing more than a buss

from those lips to her skin. And yet her pulse skittered under his mouth. "Meeting you has made an awful night a thousand times better."

The way he held her gaze, the banked fire in it...she wanted to answer it with her own fervor. For one night, she just wanted to be Amira and not a power-obsessed man's daughter, nor the fiancée of a mostly indifferent prince. She wanted to sink into Adir's arms and let him carry her away.

"You know, when you smile, you get two dimples. Did you know that dimples are caused when a facial muscle called *zygomaticus major* is shorter than normal? Sometimes, they're also caused by excessive fat on your face. Although, in your case, it's definitely not excessive fat, because you look hard as those rock structures we see in...in..."

His smile dawned as slow and bright like the sun over the horizon.

Amira buried her face in her hands and groaned loudly.

"So you're informing me that my facial structure is flawed, yes?"

She tried to tug her hand from his. He didn't let her. "Oh, please, you know you're flawless."

That seemed to take him aback. Didn't he look at himself in mirror? Did he not have women flocking to him for a glimpse of that wicked smile?

Still smiling, he pulled her to her feet. "You're… like a desert storm, Amira."

"I'm not sure if that's a compliment."

His eyes gleamed in the darkness. "Do you want a compliment, *ya habibiti*?"

"Yes, please."

Again that pure laughter—a reward for her boldness. "You're precious. Now, do me the honor of letting me check you."

When she straightened all the way, he patted her down in an impersonal manner. As if he was used to her antics and had done it a thousand times before. As if he cherished his right to indulge her.

A hard knot made its place in Amira's throat.

His hands rested on her shoulders. The sheer breadth of him took her breath away anew.

"So what was it this time?"

Caught staring at him once again, Amira frowned. "What was what?"

"What caused you to divulge all those important facts about dimples to me? Was I making you sad, perhaps? Upset? Angry?"

"You're shamelessly goading me into admitting something I shouldn't. Isn't it enough that I made a fool of myself?"

"Please, *ya habibiti.*"

She raised a brow, stalling for time. "Why do I have the feeling you never say that word?"

He shrugged. "A couple of times in the last decade."

She sighed. It wasn't as if he didn't know. "I'm attracted to you. I could steal all kinds of romance novels from the library and read about all the feelings that hit a woman when she finds a man attractive, but it's not even close to what I feel. You could be forgiven for thinking it was all cooked up to sell books, this whole chemistry thing. And yet...it's new and it's strange and it's utterly scary and it's..."

Heartbreaking and painful.

Despair swamped her so fully and so suddenly

that she pulled away from him. Looking up, she fought for composure.

Stars glittered in the sky above, winking at her. The fragrant night with its whispers and taunts seemed like a punishment now. It promised something she could never have.

Warmth coated with his scent reached her back. She tensed as he stilled behind her. Her pulse zigzagged all over at the closeness. He didn't even touch her.

"Come away with me, Amira. Just for a few hours. I promise you again I would never harm you."

"It's wrong."

"Why?"

"I'm not free to be attracted to you like this. I'm not free to indulge in this…this late-night stolen moment with you. And not just because my father would skin me alive if he found out." Longing curled through her and she tried to shut it away. "I'm a betrothed woman."

There was that contained energy within him again. Like walking too close to fire. "Is it your fiancé that…" the words choked in his throat "…that hurt you?"

"No. He…is a perfect gentleman who barely even looks at me. If you ask him what color my eyes are, I'm sure he wouldn't know."

"Then who is it?"

"My father. He…his temper gets away with him."

Whatever it was that made him cover the last step between them, she didn't care. His arms enveloped her on either side and unlocked her tight grip on the sill.

The graze of his hard chest against her back ripped open a longing inside of her. One, two, three…four seconds before she fell into his embrace. Sensations beat upon her. He was so shockingly hard all over—his abdomen against her back, his thighs resting against the back of hers, his muscular arms wound tightly around her own… He didn't press the part of him that she wanted to feel most, to her wicked shame.

And yet, she felt consumed by him.

She closed her eyes and leaned back into him. The scent of him filled her every breath. His heart thundered against her back. She rubbed her thumb over the back of his hand, curious for the feel of him.

His skin was rough and tanned, his fingers long and square-nailed. A dark emerald jewel sat on his ring finger and Amira traced it, too, carving it into memory.

It was the first time in her life that she had been held like this by a man. It was both exhilarating and comforting—just like the man himself.

"Is that why those shadows linger in your beautiful eyes? Because you love this man you are to marry but he does not love you in return?"

"Love? I would settle for acknowledgment as a person. My father is King Tariq's closest friend. I have been betrothed to Prince Zufar for most of my life." A bitter laugh escaped from her mouth. "I'm to be the future Queen of Khalia, Adir.

"I've been trained, educated, groomed, molded to within an inch of my life to complement Prince Zufar in every way. My life has never been my own. My will can never be mine. My dreams and desires…are not mine."

CHAPTER TWO

SHOCK BARRELING AT him with the might of a sandstorm, Adir struggled to hold himself still. She was Zufar's betrothed... The future Queen of Khalia!

The realization drummed in tune with his heartbeat even as desire filled every inch of his body. "You're shivering," he whispered, moving his hands up and down her arms.

Thoughts came and went through his head like sand held in a palm. His fingers must have tightened over her shoulders for she let out a soft gasp.

Adir gentled his grip, but for reasons he couldn't fathom, he didn't want to let her go.

The bones at her shoulders jutted under his palms as he tried to soothe her. And himself.

Desire for her, he understood. She was beautiful, brave, smart, funny.

But this fierce possessiveness that coursed

through his blood… It stemmed from something else.

That she was his half brother's most precious
possession perhaps? Now in his hands?

"I should walk away." Her words were a whisper in the night—a plea, a demand on herself.
Yet she didn't move from the cradle of his arms.
"From you. From this moment. It only tells me
how much I cannot have. This…" she brought
his arms up to her face, burying it in his palms.
The soft buss of her kiss against his skin burned
him "…only pains me. Only reminds me of how
much I never had. And never will have."

"Shh… I only want to hold you, Amira," he
said, even as his mind raced. "Whatever you
need, it is here, now, with me."

Turning, she burrowed into him. Her arms
wrapped around his waist, her face hidden in his
chest. The scent of her hair filled his own breath.
He wrapped thick strands of her hair around his
fingers, coiling and uncoiling, not unlike his own
thoughts.

She was so damn innocent and trusting. Such
a gift. A gift Zufar didn't deserve. A gift Zufar

didn't even value, for why else would she crave a stranger's company so much?

A gift that had unwittingly fallen into Adir's hands.

He raised her chin until she was looking into his eyes. The transparent desire he saw there banished any doubts he might have had. Feral possessiveness filled him and he touched his mouth to hers in a soft press that sent lust punching through him.

She was so beautiful and young and soft.

So easy to seduce.

If anything inside of him revolted at the idea, Adir suppressed it with a ruthlessness learned through years of surviving the harshest desert conditions.

Shocked at first, she stilled underneath his kiss. But it was already there, the heat he had felt between them, a small spark waiting to be ignited.

Adir ran his hands over her back, soothing the tremors, learning her curves, all the while gently nibbling at her lips.

Honey and heat, she was the most perfect thing he had ever tasted. An urgency he had never known before filled his blood, pounding at him to push her against the wall behind them. To lock her body against his hungry one. To thrust his tongue into her mouth while he entered her heat in the same way...to make her his, here, in this moment, to stamp his...

No!

A small voice inside him whispered. Whatever his reasons for doing this, he wanted to make it good for her, too. And that meant he couldn't let his libido run rampant.

"Adir?" she whispered, blinking owlishly. Making him smile. "Why did you stop?"

"I wanted to make it good for you."

"It is good. It is so... I didn't know a simple kiss could be so animalistic. So powerful."

For an innocent, sheltered beauty, how could she be saying the one thing that fired his blood? He dug his teeth into her lower lip. And licked it when she moaned. "Between the right couple, a kiss can be a lot more."

"So, it is this good for you, too?"

"You have quite the scientific mind, don't you?"

She shrugged, studying him with those big eyes. "I wondered."

He rubbed his nose against hers, a gesture of tenderness that shocked even him. It was only a prelude, he reminded himself. She had been his for the taking from the moment she had glanced up at him and sighed that feminine sigh.

What was wrong with blending into her fantasy a little? Giving her what she wanted? "You wondered what, Amira?"

"If it felt the same to you. I… I have never shared such a passionate kiss with any man."

"Not even your fiancé?" The question slipped past his lips.

"No. The most he has ever done is hold my hand. At public ceremonies." She blinked and he knew he would never forget that earnest expression in those wide eyes. The transparent desire. "Coming back to us… You've obviously been with a lot of women."

He couldn't remember a time he had enjoyed a conversation with a woman as much as he enjoyed having sex. But then, when had he had the inclination or time to have a proper relationship?

For him, women were for sex. To sate his body's needs. And only when he was on his overseas visits because he could not disrespect any of his own tribes by taking a daughter or a sister or another's wife as a lover.

Not when all the power rested in his hands.

"Why obviously? And are you asking?" he teased.

"No," came her resounding answer. "I think it is tacky and I really don't wish real life to interrupt this…dream. The only reason I brought it up is because it makes me curious if it feels just as powerful and passionate for a man who is sexually experienced and has had a variety of partners, in contrast to a woman who has lied to her own best friend when she told her that her fiancé had done more than kiss her because she feels too pathetic to admit that he barely even looks at her."

This time, her admission, instead of giving that high again, made his chest contract in a strange sensation. No…chemistry was a strange thing, and he didn't need to understand it. It was a tool tonight and he was using it. As he had always done—to carve his own path in life. To rise from orphan to sheikh of warring tribes.

To be the man who had done the impossible.

He brought her palm to his chest where his heart was thundering. Down his chest to the flat plane of his abdomen and farther down.

Eyes wide like a dark oasis on a moonlight, she gasped when her hand reached his groin. He covered her hand with his and let her feel the shape and hardness of him. It was a bad idea that made him grit his teeth when she explored him with that innate curiosity, her breath hitching in and out in the dark silence.

He leaned his forehead against hers, locking her wrist. "I have been like that from the moment I touched you. That kiss between us, Amira, is no common thing. It is a spark waiting to burn and I can't breathe for wanting to set it alight."

An incandescent joy lit up her face, and in that smile, he felt like a king.

Clasping her cheeks with his palms, he kissed her gently. He licked at the seam of her lips. Again and again. He sank his fingers into the thick mass of her hair and pulled her toward him until she was a perfect fit for him. He licked a damp trail from her neck to her jaw, dropping soft little butterfly kisses over her cheek, her nose, her eyelids, her temple. Everywhere but the sweet offering that was her mouth.

He did it again and again, until it felt like he had been waiting an eternity to taste her. Until every muscle in his body was coiled tightly, until the innocent rub of her belly against his erection was sensuous torture.

"I could do this all night, *habiba*," he whispered, his own contrary nature fighting the pull she had on his own control. This was a means to an end—a pleasurable means, though.

"I can't," she threw back at him, her eyes daring him.

Adir laughed and decided to give in.

She groaned into his mouth and he deepened the pressure, hungrier than he could ever remember being for the taste of a woman's lips.

No, for *this* woman's lips. *This* woman's body, her innocence and the desire she expressed with such fierceness and generosity.

Her hands caught between their bodies while

he pressed her against him. When he demanded entry into the sweet cavern of her mouth, she gave it, clinging to him with a deep moan. He licked the inner curve of her lower lip, using every ounce of skill he had at his disposal.

Her hands moved to his shoulders, her breasts pressing into his chest, her mouth so addictively hungry for more. It sealed the night.

He would give her what she desperately needed for one night. She would come with him willingly, he knew that—the fire between them, it was unlike anything he'd ever seen or felt.

"Come away with me, Amira. For one night. A few hours. Steal something for yourself from your own life, *ya habibiti*."

Her swollen pink lips trembled, her eyes shining with desire along with something else. He didn't have to ask, she was his for the taking—the pulse beating madly at her throat, the hunger in her gaze—and yet Adir wanted her to make the choice.

He would take what he wanted—revenge. He would steal something that belonged to his half brother, just as Zufar had stolen from him. His revenge on Zufar so much fuller if his betrothed came away with him out of her own choice.

If she chose Adir over Zufar even for a few hours...

"A choice, Amira," he said, running his thumbs over her trembling lips, his body primed for possession, and yet he carefully used the words that would shred the last bit of her fear and doubts, a ruthless strategy he had learned from his mother's letters. "You can go back to your bed and wonder what magic could have happened between us for the rest of your life. Or..." He bent his head and licked the pulse throbbing at her neck and felt her jerk toward him. He smiled wickedly before sucking the tender skin with his lips before releasing it with a popping sound. This time, she writhed against him, looking for relief from the ache between her legs, he knew. She was ready for him, even if she didn't know it. And the knowledge filled him with a primal pride, not unlike the rulers before him who had mastered the harsh desert. "...you can choose me. This. For a few hours."

When she kissed his knuckles, when she looked

up at him with tears shining in her eyes, as if he was the sun and moon and stars all combined together, he pushed away the fragile thread of unease in his gut.

You're a dirty stain.

He would pay Zufar back for those words. He would take what had been handed to him without guilt.

Victory thrummed through him when she said, "Yes, I… I would like to spend the…a few hours with you."

He pressed his mouth against her temple, holding her tight until the shivers that had overtaken her subsided. She was courageous, this fragile beauty, and he would make this night worth that courage. He would show her infinite pleasure.

"I will return you unharmed, yes?"

When she nodded, he took her mouth in a fierce kiss, forgetting in that instant that she was innocent. He bit the lush pillow of her lower lip and when she moaned, tangled his tongue with hers. Heat built inside of him, goaded on and on by a dark need to possess her. To take what should have been Zufar's by right.

His mother's legitimate son, the man who was poised to be King of Khalia, the man who had never doubted his origins or his place in the world, the man who even now denied Adir his rightful place when he himself held Khalia in his palm…

It was a fitting revenge.

His body vibrated with the need to be inside her, here…in the dark stairway. But whatever his half brother thought of him, Adir was no savage.

He pulled the threads of his control together and pulled away from the lush temptation of her mouth. Already, her lips were swollen and her hair mussed with his questing fingers.

And yet Amira didn't back away, her breaths falling and rising rapidly. "Where shall we go?" Her eyes shone with an impish delight, even as she shivered. "I have to return before—"

"I have heard so many tales about her gardens," he said, remembering the beautiful words with which his mother had painted the gardens. "That she toiled hours and hours there, that they were her true love."

"The Queen's Gardens? You know of them?"

He simply nodded.

A wide smile curved Amira's lips. "That's exactly where I wanted to go tonight."

He took her hand in his and led her down the steps. "Then it must be fate that I came upon you tonight, of all nights."

A small frown tied her brows and she halted his steps. Her chin tilted up, a fierce resolve in her eyes. "Not fate, Adir. No. You and I... We ended up in this darkened corridor because we both made choices, yes? Tonight, there is no fate, there is no destiny, there are no forces commanding us. Just you and me."

"You and me," Adir agreed and pulled her on, before she could see the shadow of his dark thoughts in his eyes.

She was his tonight. Not Zufar's. That was all he had to remember.

Amira felt as if she had been floating on clouds for the last two hours. Two whole hours she had spent with Adir by her side, touring Queen Namani's famed gardens. Two hours spent smiling, talking, laughing, teasing.

Two hours in which she had been more herself than she had been her entire life.

Whatever it was Adir did in his real life, it had taken him mere seconds to maneuver them both out of the stairway and through another corridor of the palace manned by armed guards.

Almost as if he had been trained in subterfuge in the military division of Khalia. Or perhaps the map of the Khalian Palace was embedded in his head, because he had known ins and outs through the lit and unlit corridors that wound down to the paths of the garden, routes that even Amira who had visited for years didn't know.

Was that it? Was he a member of the visiting guard called upon as security for the queen's funeral? Someone who traveled all over the region but never stayed still in one place?

Was Amira one of a number of women he did this with?

Seconds after the thought occurred, Amira discarded it. She didn't really care what he did or how he lived. She couldn't afford to. Not if she wanted to steal away this night for herself. Not if she wanted to believe that she deserved a few hours with a man who really saw her. Who admired her and liked her and was attracted to her.

Except for that shock she had glimpsed in his eyes when she had confided to whom she was betrothed, he hadn't mentioned Prince Zufar again. Or the royal family. Only Queen Namani filtered into their conversation once in a while. If she sensed a certain veneration in his tone for the dead queen, Amira ignored it. What she thought of Queen Namani, however contrasting to his view, was irrelevant to tonight.

This night was hers.

So she let herself be Amira and she didn't press him for any answers. Not that she doubted he would give her answers if she demanded them.

For all his charming wit and teasing taunts, there was a remoteness to him. And that was after coming up against that smooth arrogance of a man who knew he was an alpha among men. And also a protector at heart, for she had seen the fierceness of his expression when he saw her bruise.

"Cold?" he asked as she shivered at the thought and Amira nodded.

Instantly, she was surrounded by the warmth of his jacket.

Moonlight carved the deep planes of his face with an even harsher outline. Even with the fragrance of the night-blooming jasmines filling the night breeze with a pungent scent, the scent of him clung to her skin instead. They walked along the walls of the small maze until they reached the famed fountain in the center, lit up by huge brass containers holding lights.

She had visited the palace innumerable times and yet had never seen this cozy spot in the middle of the maze. There was a sense of secrecy about it, amplified by her knowledge that King Tariq had had it built as a present to please his wife Queen Namani.

Galila had never told her if her mother had appreciated it or not.

But it was a beautiful, magical night—as if the universe itself were conspiring to give Amira what she wanted.

The center of the maze felt as if it had been designed for them. The tall hedges provided privacy and the water at the intricately sculpted fountain was a tinkling backdrop that drowned out everything else.

Every sense she possessed tingled with awareness of the man holding her hand.

"Why a nursing degree?" he asked.

Warmth spread through her chest. "When I was a little girl, my mother talked a lot about how she had always dreamed of studying medicine. She bought me this cute doctor's toy set and we used to play... She would be the patient and I the doctor.

"I think she had just as much fun as I did. And then suddenly, she fell ill. I used to sit by her and study and then just like that, it seemed, she was...gone.

"I was a good student, made the top of my grade always. But when I broached the subject of studying medicine with my father, he was dead against it. Said I was destined for better things.

"Soon, Zufar and I were officially betrothed and then...at some royal dinner after our engagement, I told him that I wanted to study nursing. That it would bring a nice background to the various children's charities I would be working with in the future. And that I needed his permission to trump my father's refusal. That if he gave me his accord in that moment, I would never ever ask him for anything else for the rest of our lives. It was the only time I think he really looked at me. Not just this…placeholder of a wife that had been chosen for him, but a real, breathing woman."

"What did he say?"

There was a strange intensity in Adir's voice and Amira smile faltered. "That he…much preferred a wife who knew how to keep herself happy than one who ruined everyone else's life. He…told my father that my education, my future all belonged to him as my future husband. I could have kissed him just for that."

"Did you?"

She shook her head, trying to find again that fun, easy footing between them. An uneasy light came into his eyes whenever she mentioned Zufar. "No…even if I had, it would have been only from gratitude. Nothing like the one we shared." She couldn't imagine ever kissing Zufar like that. Ever sharing this sense of camaraderie with him. Ever feeling a fraction of what she felt with Adir even if she spent a hundred years with him.

Adir turned her toward him, his face wreathed in shadows. "For a woman who recites every inconsequential fact as if her life depends on it, a woman who looks so beguilingly innocent, you're quite cunning."

"You make me sound…wicked."

He laughed, and the sound surrounded her in waves. "You took the situation you were handed and turned it to your advantage to realize your dream. It is a compliment, Amira."

And because the genuineness of his emotion reverberated in his words, Amira went on her toes and pressed her mouth to his. She wanted his laughter and his compliments. But she also wanted to soak in the heat and hardness of his body. To learn what it was to be a woman who desperately desired a man.

She needed to be the woman who reached for what she wanted. This time, she opened up for him, like a sunflower turning toward the sun, trusting him to take her wherever he wanted.

This time, when he devoured her, she was ready and more than willing for it.

The male heat of him surrounded her, his fingers moving, touching, digging into her body, waking her up.

She clung to him, to the raw heat he evoked with his wicked mouth, to the rough urgency of his tongue as it slid in a spine-tingling dance against hers.

His fingers buried in her hair, he tugged her face up. "I would love to be there on the day when Amira Ghalib decides to be truly wicked."

She traced the outline of his lips with her thumb, the press of his lengthening erection against her belly searing her skin. "This is the moment, Adir. I want to be wicked. With you."

His dark eyes flared with fire, with need. With deep desire. "Here, with me?"

When he pulled the jacket off her shoulders and laid it on a thick grassy bank, Amira's heart pounded. When he turned her around and undid the zipper holding her long gown together all the way to the curve of her buttocks, her breath grew shallow.

When he pushed the dress off her shoulders and kissed a line down of her spine, all the way to the curves of her buttocks, she thought she would incinerate from the inside out.

And when he fell to his knees, when he turned her around to face him, when he buried his face in the flat curve of her belly, when he gripped her hips and took a deep breath as if to inhale the scent of her arousal, she gasped at the rush of wetness at her core.

When he slid his fingers through the thin strings of her panties and pulled them down, when he delved into the folds of her sex while his dark eyes held hers captive, when he licked the wetness on his finger with a wicked, all-consuming smile and asked if it was all for him, her knees refused to hold her up and she fell into his waiting arms.

If she lived a hundred years, Amira wouldn't forget the sounds, the scents, the sights of that night. Of the night-blooming jasmine he had pinched between his fingers and rubbed over her belly as he licked her before declaring that no scent in the world could beat the scent of her arousal.

Of the stars shimmering in the sky overhead because he had taken her nipple in his mouth in such a carnal caress that she had thrown her head back into the grass.

Of the throaty sounds she had made, again and again, unashamed, begging whispers when he penetrated her with two long fingers so gently that she thought she would explode for the want of more.

Of the sensations that poured through her, like buffeting waves of the sea when he thrust into her—the quick, sharp flash of pain, the overwhelming fullness when he was seated all the way in her, the feeling that she would never again be whole without him; the sweat beading on his forehead and the tautness of the lean angles of his face; the flutter of butterfly wings of pleasure in her lower belly when she shifted to relieve the fullness, the tight friction that sent arrows of sensation firing in all directions when he moved, the building vortex of need in her lower belly every time he drove into her…

She wanted to drown in the pleasure their bodies created together. She wanted to give herself over to the moment, let him cast her about as he pleased.

But for the even more desperate need to watch his face.

Silvery moonlight caressed the sharp planes, etched tight with need as he thrust in again. The grunting sound he made in the back of his throat wound around her senses. And then when he looked into her eyes, his amber eyes lit with desire, Amira pushed up onto her elbows and kissed him.

He tasted like sweat and horses and masculinity.

"You want something," he whispered and Amira nodded.

"I want to touch your skin."

He nodded.

Amira sneaked her hands under his buttoned shirt, greedy for more and more of him. Velvet rough, his skin was warm, his heart racing under her fingers. She moved her hands restlessly over his chest, discovering the roped muscles of his abdomen she couldn't see, and lower where he was joined with her.

When she snatched her hands back, he smiled. And kissed her on her mouth.

"You like this?" she asked, desperate for more of him, just as he thrust in again.

He wiggled his hips in some swirly motion and Amira's eyes rolled back. "Do you doubt it still, *habiba*?"

And then his fingers were at the throbbing spot where pressure had been building with his every thrust, and then he was rubbing and pinching in between his smooth thrusts and Amira thought she would die if she didn't...

Finally she released a thready, wicked sound when pleasure beat upon her in waves and waves.

"You're the most beautiful thing I've ever seen," he said in a husky voice and Amira's eyes flew open.

And when he moved faster and rougher inside her, when he pressed a rough, biting kiss to her mouth, when he gazed into her eyes and whispered her name as his own climax rushed him, when the indescribable pleasure he found with her laid him out in all his vulnerability, stripping from him the arrogance and the command and whatever darkness that dwelled in him, Amira knew she had made the right decision.

This man was hers, in this moment.

And she had chosen it.

CHAPTER THREE

Four months later

AMIRA TURNED SIDEWAYS and stared at her reflection in the gilt-edged, full-length oval mirror standing on clawed feet digging into the lush carpet on the floor. Everywhere around her was gilt furniture and priceless rugs and…it was all a cage.

A golden cage from which she had no freedom, a place where no one even knew the real her.

Her hands went to the swell of her stomach, utterly undetectable in the voluminous folds of her jeweled wedding gown.

Her wedding gown…her wedding day…and she was pregnant with another man's child.

Adir's child.

The thousands of gems sewed onto the tight bodice glinted in the mirror. Under the sun's rays cast into the room through the windows, the glitter of the gems reflected everywhere, even catching her in the eye every time she looked up.

At least they made the tears in her eyes look like an illusion of light. Already, her friend Galila and the maid she'd been assigned had given her strange looks when she had insisted on getting herself into the dress that weighed a ton.

But maybe she should have let them see the evidence of her one night of freedom. Maybe it would have been better if the dress had showed her growing belly.

Her father's rage when she'd told him had known no bounds. Until that moment, she hadn't realized how much the powerful connection, the status of being the queen's father mattered to him. Until that night, when he had roughly pushed her and locked her in her room, she had always made excuses for his autocratic, even sometimes violent behavior.

What did he think Prince Zufar would do when he discovered his wife was pregnant with another man's bastard? A word she hated with every inch of her being, a word her father had used again and again to drill it into her that that was what her child would be called if she didn't marry Zufar.

Ya Allah, she hated deception.

Zufar had never been interested in her, but he didn't deserve this.

Her father meant to force her to give her child away. Like an unwanted package thrown onto the streets. A stain on her reputation to be swept away…

A growl emerged from her throat, startling Galila and the maid.

Despite her father's threats, she had made every effort to see Prince Zufar alone last night. Somehow, she would have muddled through the explanation about why the wedding needed to be called off. But her father had caught her two steps away from the prince's private study where he had agreed to see her.

He had dragged her back to her room and backhanded her with such brutal force that she had lost consciousness. And by this morning, it was too late.

Prince Zufar had already left for the parade walk with King Tariq and would meet her at the hall where their wedding ceremony was to be held.

In every guard, in every visiting dignitary, in every man she came across, she had searched for those broad shoulders, that serious face. That wicked, warm smile.

She had searched because she needed a way out of her predicament, she reminded herself. Because she desperately needed to stop this farce her father was bent on having played out. Nothing else.

But there had been no sign of Adir.

"Amira…is everything all right?" asked her childhood friend, Galila—Prince Zufar's sister.

Fear made Amira's mind leap from one useless fact to another. "Did you know that the money that has been spent on the future queen's wedding dress throughout history could have fed and clothed Khalia's poor more than ten times over? That it takes three hundred days and twenty women working from sunup to sundown to create a dress like this?"

Her gaze concerned, Galila took her friend's hands in hers. "My brother might not be…the ideal man. But he's not a monster, Amira." Galila knew of her friend's father's temper and she must think that was why Amira was afraid.

Unable to meet her eyes, Amira pulled away.

Galila sighed. "The maid and I will bring the royal jewelry. Will you be all right for a few moments?"

"Yes, of course," Amira answered automatically. But ten minutes later, her panic multiplied.

Could she run away before Galila and the maid returned with the jewelry? On the way to that vast throne hall, could she claim to be sick and then steal away somehow from the palace?

The gems on the dress itself would probably pay for a few months of food and shelter. Although how far would she go weighing a ton and seriously lacking in energy? For almost a week now, she had barely kept down anything she ate in the morning.

Also, the extravagantly expensive dress would be a dead giveaway. Which meant she would have to get rid of it if she meant to escape without being seen. And to shed the dress, she needed to…

Hysteria bubbled up in her chest as she dipped her head between her knees.

She would keep her baby somehow, no matter what. She wouldn't let anyone separate them.

Just that promise to herself gave her a renewed purpose.

She was gulping down a glass of water when the catch on the huge window rattled. She frowned. It was not a windy day. In fact, Galila and the maid had both noted what a gloriously beautiful day it was to get married and she had snorted...

Her breath hitched as the top of a dark-haired head appeared outside the window. And then a hard, striking face—a face that had haunted her dreams for four months.

The intricately carved silver tumbler slipped from her hand, the loud clang of it softer than her thudding heart.

Broad shoulders. Tapered waist. Hard, powerful thighs that had straddled her hips when he had stroked himself into her, causing such indescribable pleasure that Amira was swamped with heat even now.

Amber eyes. A cruel slash of a mouth that was

incapable of infinite tenderness. Adir landed on the floor with sure-footed grace.

"*Salaam-alaikum*, Amira."

She reached for the back of an armchair, blinking rapidly to clear the fast approaching tears. It was only relief. Only relief. She repeated it like a mantra.

Adir's presence meant help. Meant she didn't have to go through with the wedding.

Why he was here didn't matter. He had made no promises and she wouldn't expect anything. But he would help her escape. And then she could make a life for her and the baby, a life that she designed for herself, a life that wasn't ruled by anyone else but her. Once she had settled into a new life, maybe she could tell him. She would not force this on him. She would not change his plans for his own life.

Maybe he would agree to visit her child whenever he was between assignments, or in the country? Maybe they could reach some...

"Amira?"

She startled, her mind a jumble of thoughts. "I'm afraid to blink for fear you'll disappear. It's not rational, I know, because *I see you*. My body remembers your scent—horses and sandalwood and…you. And yet the mind is such a powerful thing, you know? It weaves such illusions. I used to see my mother like that, months after she was gone. Hallucinations are caused by…"

"How much time is left before you marry your prince?"

She flinched at the open rancor in the question. This was not the charming, laid-back man she had given her virginity to. Something was different. Something had altered.

He wasn't smiling. No, it wasn't just the absence of his smile. He hadn't smiled a lot that night, either. It was the presence of something else in his eyes today.

A dark intensity full of shadows.

A cloud of some intense emotion…resentment? Anger? Why?

He reached her with silent footfalls. His lower lip curled into a sneer as he took in her glittering wedding dress. As if she were nothing but a fake, tawdry imitation of what the future queen should be.

When his gaze returned to her face, that resentment smoothed out for an instant. There was a flash of that tenderness she'd seen that one incredible night.

"My father will arrive to escort me an hour before," she said calmly before the hurt turned into words. "Why do you look at me like that? With such contempt?"

"I do?"

"Yes."

"I'm just wondering if the one night of illicit freedom has scratched the itch for rebellion? You're happy to marry your prince today?"

Her eyes widened, his words landing with a painful punch. "How dare you…?" Looking away from him, she swallowed the anger rising inside her.

Who was this man with such twisted words? How much did she really know about this stranger? How would he react when he learned their one night had resulted in an irrevocable consequence?

"Please… Adir. Do not presume to know what drives my decisions. Everything I do or don't do has consequences." Consequences that she was dreading telling him now. Consequences that were reaching beyond just him and her.

"Where did he strike you this time?" he asked so smoothly that Amira startled at how easily he made the connection.

Renewed shame filled her. "I was going to tell Prince Zufar that I... I can't marry him. Father... pushed me into the room to stop me. I fell and hit my head against the side table and passed out."

Such savage anger awakened in his expression that she stepped back.

"I will deal with him another time."

"You are not my champion."

"Nevertheless... You have a choice now, Amira. Will you take it?"

She knew nothing about this man except that he had given her a night of incredible pleasure. But right now, he was her only option. To escape, nothing else. And still, her heart raced. "What choice are you giving me, Adir?"

"Do you want to marry him?"

"No."

"Then come away with me."

"Now?"

A shutter flickered in his eyes accompanied by a curt nod.

"I can't tell you how…" She laughed and it was a shaky sound, utterly devoid of mirth. "For once, I don't know what to say. Although I know why I can't. You see, when our brain is hit by—"

He didn't interrupt her like her father. Just moved another step closer. Until she was swimming in that remembered scent of him.

Feelings of safety and joy and pleasure enveloped her. She looked into those beautiful eyes. He offered no assurances, he made no promises.

Yet Amira trusted this stranger with the intense eyes and brooding arrogance more than anyone in her life. He was giving her a choice. For the first time in her life, a man was treating her as a person, not a thing to be controlled or molded.

All she wanted right now was to leave this life, this palace, the prince waiting for her. To leave the life of lies that her father was intent on building. What the future held for her—and whether it involved this man—she would figure out later.

"Yes, I'll leave with you, Adir."

A vicious kind of satisfaction filled the planes of his face bringing Amira's frantic breath to a halt. Fingers clamped around her upper arm, and he was already pulling her toward the window even as his gaze scanned the room with a military precision she had noticed in Prince Zufar's bodyguards.

Then suddenly he stopped and took in her elaborate wedding dress. "Take that thing off."

Her breath stilled at the vehemence in that order. "Galila and the maid will be back—"

"You will not come away with me wearing anything that belongs to Prince Zufar. You leave everything behind, Amira…this entire life, do you understand?"

Amira frowned at his autocratic tone. "I do but—"

He simply shook his head and Amira realized he wasn't going to budge on this. A dark light shone in his eyes as he folded his arms and waited.

Her heart thudded. She couldn't change in front of him. Not when it would reveal her belly. She wasn't ready to have that discussion with him.

Not yet. Not here where Galila and the maid could walk in any minute.

"I'll change into another gown," she said into the silence, sweat beading on her forehead. "But you have to undo the zipper for me in the back."

He beckoned her with a finger.

Breath held, Amira presented her back to him. The sound of the zipper filled the silence. Her skin burned where the pads of his fingers touched her. His breath feathered over her neck, sending a shiver down her spine.

The reality of standing in front of him in daylight while she could hear the gay sounds of the parade where her betrothed was…

No! She couldn't second-guess herself now.

She held the edges of the peeling dress and sneaked behind the partition she had asked for earlier because she didn't want Galila to know the truth of her condition.

With trembling fingers, she pulled her wedding gown off, hung it up and pulled on another silky one. Just taking off the heavy wedding gown helped her breathe better. Felt like the first step in taking control of her own life. Like she had stepped out of an invisible cage that had stifled her all these years.

She stepped out from behind the partition.

Something flared in Adir's eyes, but when he spoke, he was all business. "Come, I have a Jeep waiting just outside the courtyard."

Amira joined him. As if she were a feather, he lifted her onto the broad windowsill.

Amira swung her legs over and was about to jump when Galila and the maid came back into the room, their hands full of jewelry.

"Amira? What's going on? Where are you—?" And then, "*Adir!* What are you doing here? In Amira's chamber!"

Amira's racing pulse shuddered to a thundering halt as her mind slowly processed Galila's reaction. And the recognition in her eyes.

Galila knows Adir! How? Who is he?

Adir's rough palm covered her mouth before she could form the question. His arms around her shoulders, he climbed over the windowsill.

Hanging over the ledge, holding Amira with one arm firmly around her, Adir turned to Galila, a grim smile curving his mouth. Darkness shimmered in his eyes, sending a shiver down her spine.

"Tell your brother I've not only seduced his precious bride but that she runs away with me willingly. Tell him I'm stealing away his future queen, just as he stole my birthright."

And before Amira could believe that she'd heard those words fall from his lips, much less understand them, they were both falling.

He had seduced her? To humiliate Prince Zufar?

Suddenly, the night she had spent with him looked twisted, distorted. The solid ground beneath her feet couldn't stop her world collapsing around her.

A sob clawed its way up her throat, swallowing her protest. His fingers clamped around her wrist, Adir pulled her after him.

Heart beating in her throat, Amira watched as Adir maneuvered them around the swarming guards. Sounds and sights came at her like drowning waves. The morning sun throwing off overpowering heat stole her breath. Her throat was parched, her mouth dry.

All the questions Amira wanted to ask of Adir danced on the edge of her tongue as spots swirled around her vision and she sank into the inviting oblivion.

CHAPTER FOUR

ADIR SLID A frowning glance toward Amira's unconscious form while he maneuvered the four-by-four along the rough track slowly transforming into the desert floor.

Her vibrant golden skin looked alarmingly pale, like whisper-thin parchment. Blue shadows hung deep under her eyes. Her lashes, long and thick, feathered toward those sharp cheekbones like the unfurled wings of a falcon soaring against the sky.

Innocent and sophisticated, refined and sensuous, she was truly a prize worthy of a king and he had stolen her away from under Zufar's nose. Now Zufar would face the world and his precious Khalia and its people without a bride, in utter humiliation. Just imagining the thunderous expression on his half brother's face made Adir smile.

Why wasn't she coming around?

His gaze taking in the long column of her

throat, he seamlessly took the truck hundreds of feet up a giant ocher sand mound that offered three-hundred-and-sixty-degree views of the desert floor and the border of his own region.

Khalia, Queen Namani's promises, Zufar's arrogance, the turmoil he felt every time he came near his siblings... It was all behind him now.

Here, *he* ruled.

Here, he was the master of the harshest mistress of all—the desert. Here, he had forged an identity from the ashes of the dirty secrets surrounding his birth.

Even though he had lived here for thirty-one years, the sight in front of him, the harsh beauty of it, never failed to steal his breath. Miles and miles of ripples, undulating dunes in all four directions. And against the backdrop of the desolate sight lay his own encampment. A lush mirage against the stark contrast of the stretching emptiness around it.

Here was his destiny, among his people.

Armed guards, trained not to show their obvious curiosity, stood a few feet away as he turned off the ignition. His concern quickly turning to anxiety, he walked around the Jeep and gently picked up Amira. By the time he brought her into his own chamber, water, fruits and several other items he might need to bring her to consciousness were already readied around the expansive room.

Just as he laid her down amidst colorful pillows on the divan, her eyelids fluttered open.

His knee pressing into her hip, his arms around her slender back, he stayed on the divan as she came to slowly.

Eyes so dark that they were almost black were wide in her small-boned face and their intensity pinned him to the spot. Recognition, followed by pleasure and an incandescent joy stared back at him. It was such pure, radiant emotion that it seared him through to his soul. And even as he was staggering under the impact of that, it vanished like the mirage of water under the harsh desert sun.

Wariness and fear dawned in those eyes. A breath later, she jerked away from him so suddenly that all his fighting instincts came rushing to the fore.

His entire body froze, his heart kicking against

his ribcage. He had felt something, mere seconds before she moved back. When his arm had grazed her midriff. When his palm had rested on her stomach.

A slight swell. A bump where she had been flat before. He knew because he had kissed and licked the softness of her belly, tickled it with his breaths...

Was Amira pregnant? With his child?

His knuckles turned white—rage and fear and so many things crowded him, stealing his thoughts. And if he had been an hour late, if he hadn't given in to that primal pull he felt for her against all his rational instincts, against the warnings that he was weakening for a mere woman—an unprecedented thing—Zufar would have married her.

His child would have been Zufar's under the law—to do with what he pleased.

Forever lost to him. And he would never have known.

A growl fell from Adir's mouth. "Amira—"

"No, don't!"

She was half lying down, half sitting up, her

hands fisted on both sides into the thick rugs, her breaths shallow and panting. Her eyes were panicked and out of focus. She looked like a deer caught in the sights of the predator. He was the predator she feared.

Reacting to her fear, he put his hands up, showing that he meant her no harm. And still her breathing wouldn't settle. Worse, the more her eyes traveled over him and the tent, the more her agitation increased. The upper curves of her breasts rose and fell. Her cheeks turned an alarmingly pale shade while sweat beaded on her lips.

"I can't…breathe," she whispered.

Adir pulled the knife he always kept against his leg, straddled her hips and with precise movements, cut through the bodice of the dress from the neck to just a little below her navel.

He'd always thought of himself as an educated man, a man dedicated to progress, a man determined to bring as much advancement in technology as possible to his tribes—the man who straddled tradition and progress for the betterment of his people. And yet as he cut away the dress, Adir felt like one of his desert ancestors from the stories he'd been told when he had been a boy. Of warriors capturing cities and claiming prizes and untold treasure.

A treasure was in his hands now.

"No, wait—" she begged in that panicky voice.

He didn't. Holding the knife between his teeth, he grabbed the ripped edges of the dress in his hands and pulled.

And then slowly, with carefully controlled movements that wouldn't tease his control, he got off the bed, re-sheathed his knife and only then did he allow himself to look at her.

Wavy, lustrous strands of hair fell away from the sophisticated hairstyle, falling in wispy curls caressing her face. Some ridiculous, flimsy, sheer thing made out of cream lace covered her from her chest to her thighs. Adir's breath punched up to his throat.

For four months, he had dreamed of her. Of this.

There was nothing else beneath the transparent lace. Nothing but her flesh. Flesh he had held, touched and kissed, cajoled and caressed but not seen, except in flashes and stolen glances under the cover of moonlight.

Every time he went near night-blooming jasmine, he was reminded of her. Of supple curves and soft cries and skin like silk. Of tight flesh enveloping him so completely. Of dark intimacy and indescribable pleasure.

Now, every X-rated thought and sensation he had enjoyed of that night was finally granted glorious, Technicolor vision. Nothing he had imagined could equal the ripe beauty that was Amira Ghalib.

It was only a few seconds that he took to look— dark red nipples jutting proudly through the cream-colored lace; full, high breasts that had filled his palms so perfectly that he ached to cup them again; the fragile curve of her waist, the lush flare of her hips, with jet black curls at the V of her thighs and…the clear, round swell of her belly.

Ya Allah, she was pregnant!

With a horrified gasp, she pulled the torn edges of the dress together covering it up. But he had already seen it.

A snarl escaped his mouth.

She would have been tied to Zufar irrevocably, owned and possessed, forever out of Adir's reach. *His* child out of his reach.

Another bastard denied his true parentage.

Another thing stolen away from Adir.

"Are you pregnant, Amira?" The question was eating away at him.

Her voice broke into his thoughts with a soft clang, "Is it true? You came to steal me away from Prince Zufar?"

"I said—"

Leaning against the colorful kaleidoscope of vibrant rugs that covered the wall, she looked impossibly lovely and painfully innocent. And stubborn. "Answer my question first," she demanded.

"Yes," he said, indulging her far too much, while his heart beat like a thundering tribal drum in his chest.

Color leached out from her face. "Why?"

Guilt bit into him, and he threw it off.

He had asked her and she had come with him. That his actions had been motivated by something else shouldn't matter to her. "You heard what I said to Princess Galila." It was the moment he had sensed her going utterly still in his arms on that windowsill.

She frowned, and then something dawned in her gaze. "Why did you come for me, Adir? We made no promises to each other. Four months went by after that night. And yet you appear, the morning of my wedding, a mere hour before the ceremony would begin."

"I kept thinking about you. About that night and how incredible it felt. About how I wanted to be inside you again. About how...you were caught in a situation that you didn't want."

With each question she asked, he sensed a wall being erected around her. As if she were calling layer upon layer of composure and self-possession, pushing him out. Removing the Amira of that night out of his reach. "Ah...so you came to be the hero of my story?"

The soft sarcasm jerked his gaze to her. Gone was the sweet, trusting Amira. Instead here was a woman who stared back at him with wariness and mistrust...

No matter, he told himself, as his mind made plans upon plans. What was done was done. If she was going to be in his life in a permanent role, she might as well understand that the Adir she had met that night was only an illusion he had woven to please her.

"Nothing so admirable. I did want to offer you an escape. And indulge in the passion between us a little more, if you were still so inclined."

"So you decided I would be your lover?" Her taunting words couldn't hide the color slowly seeping back into her cheeks.

His concern faded a bit.

"Yes…maybe." He shrugged. "I hadn't exactly worked out the logistics of that. My position does not make it easy for me to have lovers. At least, in a longer time frame. But I knew I wanted you and you needed escape, so it was just a matter of figuring out the optimum timing. I had a guard keep a close ear to the ground in the palace regarding the wedding to relay the news to me as needed."

"You waited, on purpose?" A flash of anger in

her eyes. "As if this…as if my life were a chess game? As if I were a pawn?"

"Strategy is my blood, the air I breathe. My libido could wait and so could you if it meant a better result."

"What result?"

"If I were to steal you away on the morning of the wedding, in front of Khalia, in front of the whole world, in front of all of his distinguished guests, Zufar's humiliation would be…complete. My revenge even more fulfilling."

"Why? Why do you hate him so much?"

"Because he continues to deny me what is rightfully mine."

If he thought the sweet Amira he had known would crumble in front of him, he was very much mistaken. "That night when you…" a betraying flash of color seeped up her cheeks, and yet she pushed on bravely, and he couldn't help but admire her composure "…invited me to spend time with you, I had, fortunately for you, confessed who I was. Had you already planned it? To have sex with me?"

Some flicker of emotion in her eyes, desperate and yearning, flashed now. Trained though she might be to weather anything as the future Queen of Khalia, her naïveté and inexperience weren't shed so easily.

Much as she tried to hide it, she was immensely hurt by his actions.

But tenderness was an affection unknown to him. He had neither the intention nor the inclination to soften the truth for her. Nothing—not her wounded big eyes nor her body—would change what he was inside, what had driven him that night to seduce her.

He was a loner. First by fate and later by design. His mother's letters had taught him early on how necessary it was to hold himself apart if he wanted to rise to achieve his destiny.

If not for her, he would have been another goat herder, a small-time rug weaver or any other average tribesman.

But by following her words as tenets, by keeping himself separate from others, by not letting emotions rule his life, he had risen to his current station in life. To heights even she couldn't have imagined for him.

If not for the queen's fiery words, he would have been content to be a simple man, a follower.

But instead, her words had spurred him on, made him a leader. Despite his low beginnings.

Even now, now that he was the sheikh of two tribes, a businessman with interests in multinational corporations, he had no close friends, no family. No women in his life who made him weak or emotional. Only advisors and people who followed his commands. Only people who filled certain roles in his life.

He depended on no one but himself. He let no messy emotions enter his life except what drove the betterment of his people and his destiny.

Just as a ruler should.

He only knew two things in life: his duty to his people and his destiny as he'd learned from Queen Namani's words for so many years. If Amira needed him to answer a few questions about their short past so that he could move on to planning their future, so that she understood her own station in life now that she was inevitably tied to him, her own part in his life, then so be it.

"Was I standing on that stairway waiting for

Zufar's betrothed to fall into my hands?" He let a smile curve his mouth. "No. Did the time I spent with you, doing what we did, add a sweet, exhilarating edge to taking the grand prize that rightly belonged to Zufar? Did I revel in stealing from him as he does from me? Am I, even now, with his runaway bride here in my tent like this, imagining his humiliation, reveling in this moment? Yes, to all."

She sank into the wall behind her as if she meant to burrow inside and disappear, one hand still holding the tattered edges of the dress closed with the other.

He clamped his hands behind him to stop himself from reaching for her. From preventing her retreat.

He wanted to uncurl her fingers gently from that silk and lay her bare to his eyes again. He needed to rip that lace off her body with his teeth and sink into her tight flesh. He desired her arms around his sweaty body, his name on her lips again. Entreating, begging, needing him.

He could banish her fear with his touch, bend

her to his will, yes. But he had tasted her willing surrender once and nothing else would do now.

"Does that answer all your questions, Amira?"

There was a faint tremble in her lithe body. Even, white teeth dug hard into her lower lip, sending a shaft of pure sensation to his groin.

"Very clearly, for the moment, yes, thank you."

"Then maybe now you can answer mine—"

And then he saw it. Perversely, it was the sun's rays filtering through the small crease in the tent. He saw the sheen of tears in her eyes. The utter defeat in the bow of her shoulders.

She dragged her breath in through her mouth in a huge, noisy inhale. Bright red painted nails scraped through her lovely hair as if tugging it would give her back her grip on herself.

He lost control of himself then.

He cupped her shoulder, meaning to pull her into his arms. He would just hold her for now. She had been through shock and once she was over it, she would acknowledge that she had chosen to come with him. He would allay all her worries—the fear she must have been living with for four months under the atrocities of her bullying father, knowing she was pregnant and unable to hide it for long.

His motivations didn't change the fact that she had chosen him over Zufar—both that night and today.

That was his true victory—that Zufar had had this woman in his possession and lost her to Adir Al-Zabah. She would again look at him with—

With a soft cry, she jerked away with such force that she almost tripped against the table with re-freshments.

"Do not cringe away from me."

Wide eyes pinned him with the regal grace of a queen even as she righted herself. She had been bred to be one—the utter elegance of it was im-bued into her every moment. "Do not touch me then."

Even as silent tears poured down her cheeks, she didn't berate him for what he had done to her. Pangs of guilt gripped him.

"You need to calm down. It's not good for you or the baby. Your panic was making you choke—"

"I think I would prefer to choke than endure your touch right now." She whispered the words—almost as if to herself. And it was that more than anything that delivered a punch to his midsection.

He advanced on her, holding onto his control by the skin of his teeth. "Shall I put that to test, *ya habibiti*?"

"It is a test I shall fail and you shall win. As unwilling as my mind is now, there are triggers in my body that sway the brain. It's millions of years of evolutionary instincts firing into action because when it comes down to it, the animal part of my brain recognizes you as the most aggressive male, the best for procreation. Neither does it help that there are other hormones at play that make me even more susceptible to you."

"So you agree that if I touched you now, if I pulled that dress off you and kissed the curve of your breast, licked my way over the satin silk of your belly to the treasure below, I shall not find you unwilling."

"No, you won't. But later, when my brain recovers from the adrenaline injected by the orgasm you give, I shall hate you. Even more than I do now."

I shall hate you...

For four months, all he had done at night was dream of her enthusiastic responses, her soft curves beneath his hard body, the inviting cradle of her thighs. He had spilled himself again and again into his own hand at the remembered memory of her soft cry as she had found her own release.

All he wanted was to reclaim her, to take her on the night she should have gone to his half brother's bed, to seal his victory. He wanted to make her take those words back.

And yet, one look into her eyes was enough to douse his feverish lust.

He was a man who thrived on control—of himself and his surroundings. This desire he felt for a slip of a girl was nothing. He would have her—again and again until the lust in him was satisfied, yes, but he would not give in to it like a green boy looking at his first nude woman.

He would not touch her until she came to him as his wife. Until she learned her place in his life.

He closed his eyes, took a deep breath and opened them again.

Eyes filled with that nauseating fear met his. He shoved away the dismay that caused inside him. Enough was enough!

It was time to take things in hand. "You are pregnant with my child."

Knuckles white from the tight grip she held on the torn edges of the dress, she stared up at him, innocence and resolve an irresistibly complex combination. "Are you so sure it's yours? What if I had stolen a hundred other nights with a hundred other strangers after you? What if there has been a parade of men in my life and in my body since that night? What if what I shared with you was so good that I didn't wait for—"

He pulled her to him, the pictures she painted making bile rise through his throat. She was his. Only his. "Do not cheapen what happened between us."

Silent tears drew wet paths on her cheeks. She looked so painfully innocent as she dabbed them away with the back of her hand. "*You* did that. Not I."

"Games do not suit you, Amira. That child is mine." His voice shook on those words. Fear clamped his spine. Fear of loss. Of all the things he had never had and now to lose this, too… "If I had been an hour late, if you had become Zufar's wife, that child, my child would have been cast into—"

Whatever she saw in his face clearly startled her. She went to him, a fierceness in her eyes. "Whoever the father of this child is in legal terms, I would never have let him or her go. Never. Adir, I love this child already. I just needed…a way out. I don't want to talk about the past anymore. I…want to look toward the future."

He nodded, seeing the truth shine in her eyes. Whatever her naïveté, Amira would be a good mother. "It is good then that we can agree on what's important."

"Then let this farce end here and allow me to leave."

"We will marry as soon as it can be arranged."

They had both spoken at the same time. Words and eyes collided, the silent room exploding with unspoken emotions.

"No." He had indulged her enough. It was time to set things straight.

Her eyes searched his, wide with shock, seeking the truth. She fell onto her haunches, that stillness turning into shivers. Before he could reach for her, she shrank away from him. Tremors overtook her slender body and she hugged herself.

Adir waited, his patience wearing thin, and yet he felt as if he was on the cusp of something.

When she raised those eyes to him again, terror shone in it. And he felt as if he fell from that cliff into some dark abyss below. Whatever had been between them, that flimsy, intangible thing, he knew it was lost.

Forever.

She looked at him as if he were a stranger, a monster.

Even as he struggled to get a grip on reality, the loss dug into him.

"Amira?"

"A minute ago, you…you were planning logistics and timing to consider me for a temporary lover. Yet now you command that we marry? I didn't want to marry Zufar. I definitely do not want to marry you."

"Neither you nor I have a choice in this matter anymore. Like you said, actions have consequences, yes? My child will not be born a bastard. I don't want a wife that looks at me as if she doesn't know me anymore than you—"

"I don't want a husband whose every word is a lie, who not only is *not* different—as I had foolishly assumed—from all the arrogant, domineering men already pushing me around, but actually hides it beneath a veneer of kindness and charm."

"I'm the same man, Amira." If only his people could hear him now—their sheikh offering an olive branch to this mere slip of a woman, when her fate was all in his hands anyway.

"The man I thought you were that night doesn't exist except in my fantastic imagination. Ordering me or threatening me will not accomplish what you want. I have years…" there was a catch in her tone and she shied her gaze away from him and swallowed "…of experience dealing with men who want to have their way no matter what. You could beat me into a pulp and I would still not surrender my will."

He reached her before he knew he had even moved. "Do not compare me to your father ever again. I'm a man of honor. What I do or don't do has consequences, Amira. People look to me for guidance. And for the final time, my child will not be born a bastard."

Something in his words pinged inside Amira's head, bringing every panicky thought to a grinding halt. Dread twisted into a tight knot in her chest as she struggled to form the question she should have asked that night.

He had talked of Queen Namani as if he had personal knowledge of her. Of Prince Zufar denying him what was his. Of honor and his station in life and strategy and logistics…

Oh, God, what had she done? Who had she tangled with?

Sweat ran down between her shoulder blades, and an invisible cage began to weave all around her again. "Who are you? Please…the truth this time."

"I didn't lie to you that night. You wanted a night of fantasy and I gave it to you."

She had been so naive, so stupid. Even though her father had prepared her for the reality of royal life from when she had been a little girl, she had still built castles in the air. She had still developed romantic notions. She had believed that fairy tale could be real, if only for one night.

"A night of fantasy, sure. And now it is time to pay the price for that night, yes? My father was right—nothing comes freely in this world. So tell me, who are you?"

"I'm Adir Al-Zabah, the High Sheikh of the Dawab and Peshani tribes. I own three multinational information technology companies. I have a degree in law specializing in international politics and land rights. I have been informed, now and again, that I possess a passably attractive face. And you're carrying my child. I shall protect you, keep you in luxury and more than anything, I would cut my hand off before I would raise it against you. Now, shall we seal the bargain, Amira?"

It felt as if the world under her feet had pulled away.

Shock settled over her skin like a cold chill while Amira stared mutely at the arrogant stranger arranging her life according to his wishes.

Adir Al-Zabah...of course, the renowned High Sheikh of the Dawab and Peshani tribes. His reputation was legendary even among the royals of Khalia and Zyria for he had single-handedly united the Bedouin tribes of this region. Warring among themselves and their way of life dying out, he had breathed new life into them by bridging the gap between tradition and progress.

Powerful, arrogant and educated, there was no equal to him in strategy and in maneuvering the volatile politics of the region. He had brought two IT companies into the cities bordering the tribes' lands in the desert—a move that had been laughed at by political critics, yet in the space of three years had provided his tribesmen with a new mode of living.

A legal dispute had been in court for decades regarding the encroachment of a local government into the lands of the Peshani—he had won the case by bringing the Dawab and Peshani together and driving the incursions out forever.

A mere thirty-one years old, he already was a ruthless leader and a cutting-edge businessman. He was a herald of a new age for the tribes—of not only survival, but economic thriving.

She had thought they were similar souls looking for a connection in their lonely lives. He was no more lost or lonely than the lion was lost in the jungle. No less ruthless than her father or Prince Zufar in how unscrupulous he had used her naïveté and trust.

And they had no more in common than she and Prince Zufar had.

He was another controlling man who thought nothing of her own wishes or dreams.

"No. I will not marry you."

A muscle jumped in his jaw. Clearly, he was not used to being denied anything. "It is high time to let go of your foolish dreams, Amira. Do not make me take away your choices."

"It's not much of a choice if it is the only option, is it?"

She thought he would be furious, he proved she didn't know him.

He stared at her for so long that Amira wondered if the loud thunder of her heart echoed in the room.

And then he smiled. It was the smile of a predator. Of a man who always got what he wanted. Of a man who had ruthlessly seduced her while he had planned her betrothed's humiliation.

"I thought you would be happy to be free of your golden cage. Free of all the expectations and burdens that were thrust on you. Free of Zufar's indifference and your father's brutality. This is the result of a choice you made. So live with it."

"No! You—"

"Enough!" Adir said, losing his control.

Her rebellion was of the insidious kind. It was there in the defiance in her eyes, the upward tilt of her chin as her slender body cringed away from him.

It was the impression she gave. She was small and slender with exquisite curves in all the right places and yet if he closed his eyes now, all he would see would be the bright shining light of her will. Of her determination.

But much as he tried to suppress it, he had to admit there was a niggle of shame. A looming sense of…something he couldn't even recognize. And the unknown quality of it made his voice harsh, his words cruel.

"Will you now act as if I forced you into it all, Amira? You proved that you have no loyalty toward Zufar when you slept with me. You were more than desperate to—"

"You would shame what I gave you honestly? I don't care what you or my father or the entire damned world thinks. I *gave* my body to you. You think I was overcome by fear, that I wanted escape—?"

"Why romanticize it when it's exactly that? You used me and I used you," he said bluntly, even knowing that her inexperience, her sheltered worldview would never see it that way. Her father might have reared her to be a queen—to play politics and games—but there wasn't a malicious bone in her body. But she had to learn fast if she wanted to survive life with him. "Wasn't it payback, too, on your father for his cruelty, on Zufar for not giving you enough—?"

"No! Don't you dare tell me why I did it." For the first time that day, he heard pure steel in her voice. In a matter of seconds, she had transformed from a sweet, innocent temptress to a tigress breathing fire. "Your own twisted motivations color mine. I…was attracted to you. Something about you made me realize a woman's desires for the first time. That I wasn't just a pawn to be used. I *chose* to let you kiss me. I *chose* to let you give me pleasure. I *chose* to give myself one night of escape in your arms. All my life, I fought to make choices of my own within the few parameters I was allowed. That night, I chose you. And neither you nor my father nor the world—no accusations, no shame heaped upon me, no force on this earth—could take that away…the choice I made…from me."

"Then now it is time for us both to live with the consequences of that."

She was nothing to him.

No, she was not nothing to Adir.

She was used to being nothing all her life. She

had been nothing before—an object of indifference and neglect to Zufar. But his indifference had mostly left her unharmed.

She had been a means of attaining wealth and power for her father. A pawn to be used for gaining advancement. Even as she had hated it, somehow, Amira had used that to her own advantage. She had time and again persuaded her father that her education, her training to be a nurse, the charity work she did with poor women and women without healthcare, all of it increased her worth as a queen.

She had wielded her betrothal to Prince Zufar as a weapon to achieve her biggest dreams, all within the constraints her father had laid down on her.

But not once had either of them been allowed to touch her heart.

She had endured whatever they had thrown her way but hadn't let them touch the core of her.

What Adir had done to her, what he had stolen from her—oh, she had given her virginity happily enough and she still couldn't regret it—but what he had stolen from her was so much worse.

She had allowed him into her heart.

He had been the first man who had ever made her feel safe, cherished, wanted. And all her life, Amira had never been cherished.

For the first time in her life, she had seen herself as something other than a pawn. He had given her a taste of utter happiness…

Amira sank to the floor when he walked away without another word. Tears filled her eyes and for the first time since she had learned of her pregnancy, she couldn't stem their flow.

She should think of her child, she should think of its future.

And for her child, she would marry him. But she would never again trust him, never again be so naive as to believe that charming facade.

He would be her husband, the father of her child, he would have ownership of her body, her mind, her thoughts, but never her heart.

Never again would she forget that the man she was marrying had no heart.

CHAPTER FIVE

"HOW ARE YOU feeling today?"

Amira jerked up from the bed. Her scrambled movements only made the man staring at her frown.

No, he wasn't just a man.

She needed to see him as he truly was—a powerful man used to getting his own way. She had lived her whole life dealing with such men and yet quietly achieving her own way. She would this time, too.

Now that she had made and accepted her decision, relief filled her. Even being the Queen of Khalia couldn't have done what Adir had done for her. She was free of the controlling grasp of her father and that was a good thing.

Having lived with her father's constant belittling and control, Adir's arrogance and dominance was nothing. If she had learned one thing from her father, it was that every relationship had a power exchange.

And while she had always been the one with less power in all of her relationships, there had almost always been something to bargain with. Leverage.

And she desperately needed to find what that was when it came to Adir.

"Amira?"

An edge of impatience crept into his tone. For three days, he had wisely left her to stew in her own company.

But she had never been alone, for one or another woman had kept showing up. First to look after her health, she had been told. Then the lovely, funny Zara had shown up to keep her company. And lastly, the old woman Humera.

She shoved away the bitter answers that rose to her lips one after the other. "I have made peace with my fate. And nothing is wrong with my health. But I still do not like you," she said, opting for honesty.

"Look at me when I speak to you."

Exhaling a deep breath, she turned. "Yes, Your Highness."

And just like that, all her reassurances and promises fled.

Awareness filled every pore as those amber eyes watched her with that thoroughly possessive leisure.

He was dressed simply in white robes that suited the desert today. His head was covered by a red and white scarf to keep the heat at bay. His face gleamed dark gold after a morning in the sun, his potent masculinity taking over the tent.

Even having spent two days in his luxurious tent, even having spent two restless nights in the vast expanse that was his bed; even after woman after woman bowed, scraped and saw to her every need as if she were indeed a queen; even as she heard the respectful whispers and the widening amazement in her helpers' eyes when they spoke of him, the reality of it all had still eluded her.

Until now.

She looked at the arrogant angles of his face,

his air of command, the way his broad shoulders and lean strength filled the very air around her and could not believe she had been so bold as to have kissed him, to have asked him to make love to her, to have seen him in that moment where he had lost all control of himself. An utterly useless rush of power filled her.

His desire hadn't been faked—this realization that had been simmering under all the other overwhelming facts rose to the fore.

Was that her leverage? Did he still want her—or was she simply the spoils of war, a convenient receptacle to carry his future dynasty?

She licked her lips and saw his eyes flare.

A muscle twitched in his jaw. "I have spent all morning resolving ridiculous disputes pertaining to goats and cattle and what not. Do not test my patience, Amira."

"If you have one of your lackeys draw up a list of dos and don'ts dictating my behavior with you, I shall learn it by heart. What is it that you expect me to provide you with?"

"Other than the obvious?" He moved into the tent with an economic grace that meant Amira couldn't help but stare. A dangerous glint appeared in his amber eyes.

He ran a finger over her jaw so gently that Amira instantly closed her eyes to savor the feeling.

Fiery heat claimed her skin though the temperature fell rapidly with the sun setting outside. Because even with the chaos he had brought to her life, not one single night had passed when Amira had not wished for him beside her on the bed.

Instead, she moved away from him. "I see the speculation in the maids' eyes. Move me to a different tent."

"You give orders like a queen. And they only look at you that way because I haven't yet declared that you're their future sheikha."

She tilted her chin up. "Believe me, that's the last thing I want to be. If I had known who you were that night, I would've screamed the palace down to get away from you. I would have—"

"You're telling yourself lies. But since it probably makes you feel better, I shall leave it so."

The infuriating, arrogant beast! Was he right?

Would she have been attracted to him even if she had known what a powerful man he was?

When she had learned the truth three days ago about his identity, she had been in shock, disbelief. But now she wondered how much Adir had really wanted her that night? And how much had been the need to humiliate Zufar?

She sighed, realizing even now that she was looking to put a romantic spin on that night.

"I ran away with you because I needed a way out. But now that the wedding day has passed—"

"He will not take you back, Amira. I have received news."

Amira thought it was a throwaway comment, meant to shame her again. Meant to remind her that she had turned her back on Prince Zufar and that life.

But beneath his penetrating look, something else lingered.

Where was the man who had been so kind and approachable that night? Whose eyes had been full of pleasure and warmth?

"From…the palace? From Khalia?"

"Yes."

For two days, all she had seen of Adir was in discussions outside her elaborate tent. Two women had always been with her and a battalion of guards outside the tent. And as of an hour ago, ten men had been whittled down to one.

That same look—a sense of victory—gleamed in Adir's eyes.

He had been guarding her, she realized now, against Prince Zufar. Assuming he would come to take her back. He hadn't been willing to take the chance of her returning to Prince Zufar and Khalia.

What did that mean? Did he truly want her? Or was she still only a prize he had stolen from Zufar?

"Is there any word from my...my father?" she asked, even knowing that he must loathe her by now for everything she had thrown away, for what she had cost him.

"No. It seems he has washed his hands of you." If there was any tenderness in his tone, she didn't let it move her. Pity was not a good substitute for anything genuine like respect or affection.

"Prince Zufar...is he...?"

"He has replaced you with, of all women, a maid. The man who called me a dirty stain on the name of his house, the King of Khalia, is now married to a palace maid."

Zufar had been forced to marry the maid to save face? What had he thought of her running away with Adir? Had Galila worried for her?

Amira plopped down onto the divan, her knees giving out. For so long, her every breathing moment had been to prepare to be queen. Her fate had been tied to Zufar's.

Of course her disappearance mere hours before a dynastic wedding would have repercussions. At least Adir had made it clear that she was leaving of her own accord.

The connection had been severed the moment she had decided to jump out of the window with Adir, yes, but now…it was as if a crushing weight had been lifted.

Amber eyes locked with hers and any relief she felt was forced out of her.

Arms at his sides, powerful legs sprawled in front of him, he was very much king of the desert.

Heavy, sluggish warmth pooled low in her belly.

Waiting. Watching for every nuance on her face. In that penetrating stare, Amira saw that he wasn't sure of her. His question next confirmed it.

"Are you regretting running away with me? Giving up the queen's life?"

For three days, she had contemplated the question and come up with an answer: no.

The scales had fallen from her eyes but she still couldn't regret running away with him. Couldn't regret that night. Maybe she was as foolish and useless as her father had always called her.

She sighed. "Prince Zufar replacing me with any woman is not a surprise. I'm just...relieved that my foolishness didn't cause him unfixable damage. His indifference toward me did not deserve the humiliation I helped you wreak on him."

"It is a little late to show loyalty toward him."

His fingers closed over the engraved handle of a knife and slowly he peeled off the skin of a piece of fruit. When he sliced a small section and handed it to her, Amira shook her head.

"You chose me. Over him."

"Haven't you crowed about it enough?" She rolled her eyes and the beastly man simply smiled.

Amira breathed harder, faster as he pushed off the chair, another piece of apple held in his hands.

He smiled and in that pure devilish movement, she could see her downfall.

He lifted the piece to her mouth, slow desire making his eyes shine with a brilliant glow.

Here was the answer to her question.

Mesmerized, Amira opened her mouth. He slid the piece between her lips. The pads of his fingers lingered over her lips. She licked his fingers. The sweet and tart taste of him flew like liquid lightning to the place between her thighs. The spot he had touched that night, the spot she had tried to find to relieve the ache he caused…the spot that was throbbing now.

Trembling with need, she sank her teeth into the pad of his thumb.

His chest fell and rose as she sucked the tip into her mouth. His eyes darkened. And when she sucked it between her lips, a sound escaped his mouth—the same low, throaty growl he had made when he had spent himself inside her that night.

Amira jerked away from him, her heart racing. Her breath still uneven.

He wasn't gloating when she looked at him.

She stood at the window, looking out into the red expanse of the gorge and valley beside her when he started talking again.

"See what happens when I simply come near you. You forget all your objections. You look at me as if you're desperate for my touch, eager for me to be inside you."

He said it in such a matter-of-fact voice. As if they hadn't been ready to tear each other's clothes off.

While she...she was still shaking from the depth of her need.

Of course, she and Galila had talked about sex—without mentioning her brother specifically because that made the both of them nauseous—and how a woman's libido could be just as strong as a man's. But it all had been a theory.

She hadn't ever thought that those urges would overwhelm even her mind.

"This attraction between us…it is an added bonus," he said almost thoughtfully.

"An added bonus?"

"I like sex and I like to have a lot of it. But I also intend to remain faithful to my wife. From what I remember of that night, and from the way there's a spark in the air every time I come near you, you're explosively responsive, and like everything else, you're extremely curious about this. The things I could teach you, the things we could do together… The kind of chemistry we share would last a long time. Enough to keep me interested."

She turned instantly, disbelief skating through her.

He looked back at her steadily, his lean face a study in beauty.

If her heart beat any faster, it would jump right out of her chest. "What are you saying?"

"That we could have a more than satisfactory marriage. Zara and Nusrat couldn't stop singing your praises, even though they're prejudiced about any woman that is not from the tribes. Even Humera is impressed by you and she has never given her approval to a single woman in the tribe."

"Humera is the old woman—the midwife who came to see me?"

"Yes."

"Zara told me she never ventures out of the camp. Why did she come here?"

"I asked her to take a look at you."

"Why?"

"Because you look pale and unwell." His gaze swept over her, but this time there was no mocking smile or taunting desire. A flash of concern shone in it. "You have dark shadows underneath your eyes, and I could break you with one hand."

When he raised a brow, she hurried to reply, "I do not want to be seen as a victim. Whatever my father did, I never let it change me. It shouldn't change how you see me."

He nodded, granting her a privilege. "After two minutes with you, no one could think you were a victim. Amira, I would have you enter this marriage with an open mind. You wield your silence like a weapon, your hurt like a…shield for all the world to see. Vulnerability like yours…"

Longing ripped through her. Here was a man who saw her, who…understood her. An urgency like she never knew gripped her. As if she had to grab onto something before it disappeared.

"I thought you were no different from Zufar or my father. I was wrong."

The hesitation in his gaze made her cover the distance between them, a glimpse of the vulnerability she'd seen that day pulling her like a rope. "How am I different?"

"Zufar couldn't care less whether I was happy or sad. As long as I did my duty and didn't cause scandal, I could do whatever I pleased. My father, as long as I presented myself befitting the status of the prince's betrothed, he could not have cared less if I was rotting with misery on the inside. But you…you care that I am happy about this. Admit it, Adir, you feel guilty for deceiving me. Admit that you felt something that night."

"You're determined to see me as a knight in shining armor. I'm not."

"And you're determined that you will kill whatever you felt for me."

"Enough, Amira! Stop wearing your heart on your sleeve. Your vulnerability is a weakness. A naive, trusting sheikha is a dangerous thing. There will be many who will court your goodwill, who will use that against you. For a woman who has been brought up by a beast of a father intended for a royal life, you're far too innocent. That is the only downside I see in this."

Her heart sank. "The only downside?"

"In marrying you."

If he had slapped her, she would probably have been hurt less. "Then don't. Don't marry me. You can still see our child. I'm sure there is no shortage of women queuing up to be your bride. In fact, I'm surprised. Doesn't a powerful man like you have a girlfriend or two tucked away?"

"I thought it was tacky to mention my past relationships."

"You're the one who keeps reminding me to leave fantasy behind and live in the real world. I have accepted that you're a flesh and blood man with clay feet like the rest of us. So tell me, Adir, how many mistresses will I have to deal with?"

His jaw tightened, and anger flashed in his gaze for the first time. Only then did Amira realize how flat and unemotional he had been so far. "I told you I intend to be faithful to my wife. And I will expect the same, Amira."

When she didn't answer, he tilted her chin up. "I will not tolerate even the thought of you straying."

Even as he commanded her, vulnerability shone in his eyes. This was important to him. This was personal.

Amira met his eyes, searching for that man who had laughed with her. Wondering what lay beneath that command and duty. "Do you really believe I'm the sort of woman who would cheat on her husband? One who would bring such…discord, and invite such pain into so many lives?"

Her breath hung serrated in her chest while he studied her. "You spent a night with me while betrothed to him."

Amira felt as if he had slapped her. Tears rose

to her eyes and she struggled to blink them away. "Wow. You will use that against me again and again, won't you? For the last time, Zufar was chosen for me. Zufar didn't even know me. He had no right to my feelings."

"And I do?"

She nodded. As much as she didn't want to. "More fool me, but yes. Even before I learned that there was to be a baby. I don't think you'll ever realize what you meant to me that night. *Just* that night."

His hands fell on her shoulders, his gaze so serious. "Amira, all I mean is that you could fall in love with some man later and justify your affair. Love makes people weak, it makes them hurt others. With no thought to consequences. It's the same for men and women."

"You speak as if you have seen this."

He shrugged and looked away. Amira had the eerie sense that she had been close to learning what made him so...remote. So cynical. So alone, even. As if a bright glittering star had been within her reach and she had let it slip without even knowing.

"As little experience as I have with it, that is not love," she said. "That is…selfish indulgence."

"For someone so young and untested and so… innocent…" his knuckles ran down her cheeks, sending a thread of warmth through her "…you have very decided opinions."

"I just know there are some lines I wouldn't cross. Things that I could never live with. And since you insist on this wedding between us, it would be nice if you knew that, too."

"No, you would not be a wife who would cheat on me. You might, however, twist a knife in my gut if I did."

It looked like he knew her well enough after all. Amira laughed and automatically leaned toward him to kiss that sexy mouth.

When he stilled as she leaned toward him, she caught herself. And looked away.

And because she didn't want this awkward moment stretching any longer, she said, "So what about your history of lovers?"

He cleared his throat even as his eyes danced. "The tribes are very conservative socially. The last thing I could do is import a girlfriend from the city just to satisfy my…needs. Neither could I carry on with a woman from the tribes because that's a blatant abuse of power. So I have always kept my…associations short and un-messy. A man like me has no allowance to be emotional in his personal life anyway."

And with that pithy sentence, he revealed so much of how he saw himself. Amira frowned. He made it sound as if it were a necessity to be alone to be a ruler. As if relationships were nothing but weaknesses. "You mean you have never had a girlfriend?"

"No. And since I'm thirty-one years old, my council has been encouraging me to marry for years to establish my line. But until now, I never met the right woman that made it a worthwhile proposition. A woman I could tolerate."

Every word out of his mouth was a tempting pitfall. Every look he cast her a tug on her senses. Her heart should not race like one of her father's thoroughbreds at the thought of being his wife. At the thought of spending all her nights in his beds. But the foolish muscle did.

One. Two. Three. Four. Five.

"And I make it a worthwhile…proposition? Is this your way of wooing me?"

He shrugged, putting paid to any such notions. "You were bred to be a queen. You're beautiful, sophisticated, a consummate asset to a business-man in the outside world. Education, polish, your charity work, even your career, everything about you is an asset to a man in a powerful position. Especially me."

"Especially you? Why?"

"I'm forever caught between progress and tra-dition and you understand both. You're manipu-lative, just like me, maybe just subtler in the way you go about it. You're a survivor, Amira."

He didn't even see his actions toward her as wrong. He thought she would be an asset. As if she were a piece of equipment or an accessory.

"I will be an asset as a sheikha. I will give you a good time in bed. I will be a good wife. And what is it that you give me, Adir?"

His usually cynical gaze was filled with con-fusion and a bitter laugh fell from her mouth.

"It seems all the benefits are yours. What do I gain of this marriage?" Chin tilted up, shoulders square, she faced him. "Why would I exchange one ruthless man for another? One prison for another? Tell me why you would make a good bargain for me. Why I should throw myself into this?"

A dark smile shone in his eyes. He seemed to admire her show of backbone, her clinical reduction of this thing between them into a transaction. He took her hand in his and before she could think to object, pressed a soft kiss to the underside of her wrist. Sensations sparked inside her. "I should not forget one fact."

"What?"

"That you're a fast learner." The wealth of meaning in those words sent her hurtling into a rush of remembered sensations and words so intense that she burned all over.

Widen your legs, Amira... Tilt your hips up when I push in... Hold on, habiba.

He had been a consummate teacher and she an eager pupil.

Could she teach him some things, too? Could there be more to this marriage?

Not love, no. Maybe they were both far too realistic, but perhaps they could have a good marriage.

* * *

Her straightforwardness made Adir smile. She was a lioness, slowly coming into her own. Suddenly, the prospect of Amira as his sheikha, of having her in his bed for the rest of his life, seemed less like duty and more a thing to look forward to.

She would be such a challenge—everything she gave would have to be earned. And when her surrender came, it would be so much sweeter.

And when she did give her all to this marriage, there would be no turning back. He would have a true partner, a woman he could share so much with.

For the first time in his life, he could have an actual relationship.

"With me, you could have a marriage of respect and desire. With me, you would be free of even the shadow of your father, forever. With me, you could have a position of power as the sheikha, you could make a true difference in women's lives. With me, you will have a place to belong, Amira. If only you can summon the courage to grab it with both hands."

"Will you give me the freedom to make my own choices?"

"Within reason, yes."

"Our child," she began, "if it's a girl—she will be allowed to study, pursue a career of her own choice and will not be used as a bartering tool to move up in the world."

He raised a brow, the very picture of masculine arrogance. "What will you do if I promise all this and don't keep my word?"

"That you ask that question instead of giving me a blind promise is enough, Adir." His smile told Amira she was right.

What Adir thought of himself and what she thought of him were eons apart. Yes, he had deceived her. But from what she was learning of him, honor was important to him, too. And this child was important.

And any man who wanted to be a good father had something to recommend for himself, didn't he?

"All I ask is that anything that concerns our life, we decide together," she said. "And that you don't force me into any other role except a wife and a mother."

"The tribes will call you their sheikha."

"I can live with an honorary title. Because I already have a career, Adir."

His jaw took on a resolute tilt, his eyes gleaming. "That, *ya habibiti*, is not negotiable. You will be my sheikha, my wife, the mother of my children, and anything else I decide you should be."

He turned to leave and then stopped. "And if it's a boy, Amira?" Something shimmered in his eyes and in that wealth of emotion, Amira knew she had made the right choice even then.

The Adir she had trusted that night was a part of the sheikh, too. And that made her non-choice feel like a very real one.

"If it's a boy, I hope you will help me in raising him to be a good man, Adir. A man who is secure in who he is, a man who knows his roots, a man who understands that his life is full of love," she said on a wild risk. Her heart felt as if it had clawed into her throat as he stared at her. "Yes?"

It was not a trick of light, she knew. It was emotion that glittered in his beautiful eyes.

He nodded, perhaps because his throat was full of emotion just as hers was. At least, Amira wanted to believe so.

"And Adir?"

"Yes, Amira?"

"If it's a boy, I hope he would be as handsome as his *abba*."

The smile he left with dug grooves in his cheeks and Amira went to bed with a smile on her own. For the first time since the night she had met and chosen the man who was to be her husband.

She had thought him hardhearted, remote, a monster. But neither was she simply naive or any of those things he thought her.

She was a lot of things made up together— apparently, even a little bit foolish.

Nothing in life was simple. Not the least of which was Adir Al-Zabah.

CHAPTER SIX

THEIR WEDDING TWO weeks later was a small, private affair—a fact that Amira ended up loving—attended by councilmen from the tribes that Adir was sheikh of, her father and a handful of Adir's close friends and business associates.

He hadn't asked her what kind of a wedding she wanted. Amira had even been surprised that he'd told her that it was to be a rather simple affair since the tribes' elders didn't believing in stepping foot in the city—even for their sheikh's wedding.

"It wouldn't be the elaborate affair that you were expecting with Zufar," he taunted her.

"I would be more than glad to stand in front of the imam with you, just the two of us, and get it done."

A devilish brow arched, he said, "Neither do they want to miss my wedding. It is an occasion they've been waiting years to celebrate."

Amira sighed. Did he think she missed all the fripperies and extravaganza of her royal wedding? Nothing had been her choice—not even the dress. "Even as a young girl, I knew my wedding would never be about what I wanted. Please don't feel the satisfaction of thinking you're taking away something I long for, Adir."

The man never did what she expected. Instead of anger, he laughed, the pad of his thumb tracing the line of her jaw. "You're developing quite the tart tongue, hmm?"

And then, before she could respond to that, he pressed that sinful mouth to hers.

Fingers crawled into her hair, tilted her head up for his pleasure. The taste and scent of him rushed over her, her body rocking into his.

Such pure sensation. Such naked heat. His lips firm and soft, brushing over and over against hers; his chest crushing her breasts. Her belly bearing the press of his arousal.

Hard. Fast. No gentling, no giving, it was a furious, carnal taking. The skillful pressure of his lips pushed her lips against her teeth until she had to open for him, until tasting him was the only thought in her head.

How had she forgotten how seductively he kissed? His kiss betrayed the urgency of his desire—for days after that agreement, he had not visited her again.

Even when he had driven her to the city for a checkup and the doctor had congratulated them both, he had been thoughtful, his gaze lingering again and again on her face. His fingertips had barely brushed her skin, and that only when necessary. As if he couldn't tolerate being near her.

Finally, Amira couldn't bear it any longer. "What have I done now? You have become remote again."

"Did you send Zufar a letter?"

"Did you intercept it?" she countered, suddenly his attitude making all the sense in the world.

His nostrils flared, a tic throbbing in his jaw. Amira would have laughed if she could corral the disconnect between her mind and body. Whatever his birth, Adir Al-Zabah was every inch a royal who could command as easily as breathe.

Every time she mentioned her own mistrust for

him, a certain aloofness descended in his eyes. She could almost hear the command he stifled by sheer self-control. *You can't mistrust me, Amira. As your husband and your overlord, I command you to like me.*

If she weren't so sure of his arrogance, she would have thought that instant reserve hid his dislike of remembering his twisted motivations, even his own confusion that he had behaved less than honorably toward her.

She killed the thought as soon as it was born. One mistake in thinking she understood him and his motivations and his feelings was allowed. Doing it again was sheer stupidity.

"My guard asked me if I wanted it intercepted."

"I merely sent my apologies, Adir. He deserves more from me. After what I did."

His jaw tightened. "And is that it?"

"I wrote to Galila, too. She must be worried about me. I have heard news that she, too, is to be engaged soon."

Just as she assumed, those shutters came down in his eyes. "No note for Prince Malak?"

"Will you always mistrust me like this? Should

I question where you have been for a whole week? Should I question why you are keeping your distance from me?" But it was only after she asked the question did she realize that maybe it had nothing to do with her. It had to do with the royal family.

But every time she tried to bring up this…feud between him and Zufar, he tuned her out.

"You will cease your communication with the royal family."

"Galila is my friend. My only friend for a long time." When it didn't look like he would relent, she took his hands in hers, even if he was unwilling. "Adir, what is the harm in my asking after her? I promise there is nothing about you in those letters. Except a small reassurance that I am safe and happy, given the circumstances."

After what felt like an eternity, he nodded. This time, Amira couldn't catch her impulse in time. She pressed her mouth to his. And with a growl, he took the kiss over until she couldn't even breathe.

His touch, his kisses were fire. It was as if he forgot the resentment, the polite courtesy, it was as if he reveled in her surrender. Like he had done the first evening when they had met.

The hunger he felt for her—the reluctant slide of her tongue against his as he plundered her mouth, his powerful body shaking around her. To keep from pooling into a puddle at his feet, she grasped his shoulders. And the tight clench of his muscles under her hands as she dueled her tongue with his, as she sucked on the tip the way he did with hers brought shallow breaths and thundering hearts. Amira gasped for breath.

He placed a palm over her throat and chest, the heat from it searing her bare skin. Her breasts ached with a languid heaviness that reached right to the tips of her nipples—so close to his fingertips. Her fingers dug into his shoulder muscles. Pleading, almost begging.

"Is this what you're missing?" He didn't move his hand, didn't give her what she needed. Only watched her with a hooded gaze.

"Yes," she admitted, heat streaking her cheeks.

He roughly thrust his fingers through his hair. To stop himself from grabbing her, she knew. A thread of feminine power whispered through her at how easily this…thing between them teased his control.

A harsh smile bared his white teeth. His thumb traced her lower lip. "I want you just as much as you want me." With precise movements, he pushed her away.

"I have been alone for a long time, Amira. I cannot and will not account for my whereabouts to you on every hour at the top of the hour." That he had even answered her question took the bite out of his flippant answer. "And as to why the distance…if I come into that tent, I will be inside you within minutes. Damn it, I cannot sleep for wanting you. But you're to be my wife, the sheikha, and I can't dishonor you and myself by flouting the tribe's traditions so openly."

This was what he had meant by straddling tradition and progress. Amira gazed at him, her heart full of admiration. It took a truly complex man to respect something he clearly didn't agree with.

"I never want the tribes to question your honor. To disrespect you. And if that means a cold dip in the oasis that turns my balls blue until the wedding, then so be it."

Amira didn't know whether to laugh or cry. For she, too, missed him—missed the warmth of his kisses with an increasing ache. She went to him and buried her face in his chest, willing him to hold her. Just for a minute.

To let her pretend, even as she knew she shouldn't, that he was the Adir of that night.

"The more I learn of you from the camp and its people, from Zara and Nusrat and Humera, the more my respect for you grows. As a sheikh, as a leader, as a man who straddles past and future and owns the present...you're exemplary. But I guess it is too much to ask that a man be a paragon, an expert in all walks of life."

His fingers sneaked into her hair and he tugged at it sharply. "And what do you mean by that?"

She gasped and looked into his eyes. The eyes that she could drown in when they were smiling like now. "You could have simply informed me of your decision. But then I learned that you have shouldered responsibility since a very young age and it's clear your personal life—your interpersonal skills with women—have suffered for that."

"You're the first woman to have complaints, *ya habibiti*."

"Cheap shot, Your Highness. But if it's true, it's because I'm the first woman who dares be honest with you."

Humor twinkled in his eyes, his fingers cradling his jaw. Another tell—she was learning. He did that when he was amused despite himself. "I don't think I've ever been so thoroughly insulted and complimented in the same sentence."

Should it be another victory for her—small though it was—that even amidst the bitterest argument with her, Adir laughed? That she saw a glimpse of the man who had held her so tenderly?

If she wasn't careful, her entire identity would be constructed on what he thought of her.

"You will laugh and cry and do whatever emotionally overcome brides do at our wedding, Amira. I will not have Humera demanding of me again why my betrothed writes secretly to a man I loathe, and why she is not filled with joy at our upcoming nuptials." The arrogant lord that he was, he completely ignored her outraged gasp with a flick of his hand.

"The last thing I need is for the tribeswomen to complain to their husbands that I am forcing you into this and sullying my reputation. And yours in that process."

Of course, that was why he had come to inform her about the wedding. Not because he wanted to. Not because he considered her his partner in this, whatever his proclamations about her being his sheikha. Just like every other man she had dealt with, he meant to give her freedom only within the parameters he set for her. "And if they complained to their husbands, would it have any effect?"

He frowned. And then released a breath. "I forget how little of the world you have seen. The tribes are based on a very clear hierarchy, but women have their own power. Your father…has twisted your views of men."

He was right. The tribes' way of living—hard and with little comfort to the naked eye—was strange in her eyes. But already she had seen the close-knit community it was.

"Why does Humera have such...sway with you?" The old midwife had no family to speak of, was a font of knowledge on old medicinal remedies and the desert tribes and commanded the sheikh with the lift of a single brow. Amira had spied the genuine affection in Adir's eyes when he spoke to Humera.

"She raised me."

"And your parents?"

"My mother and Humera came from the same city. She trusted Humera to raise me when she had to give me up. As a days-old infant. So she sent me to the tribes here where Humera had settled."

To be sent away as a little infant to this harsh landscape...not to know where one had come from.

Amira wanted to ask more. It was all tied to what he had demanded from Zufar, she knew. Whatever Adir's past was, it had shaped him in life. And it was her child's legacy and a part of her life, too, now.

"Who...who was your mother?"

But she knew the answer before he gave it. In

fragments and pieces from their conversations, the truth had sunk in, without her even realizing it.

The way he had tilted his chin, something in the way he had trained those eyes on her—a glimpse of Galila that caught her breath. The veneration in his tone that night and every time he spoke of her.

"Queen Namani. I was born of an affair. King Tariq quietly arranged to send me away to Humera."

Zufar, Malak and Galila…he was their half brother! That was why Galila had known him. "And your father?"

His features tightened. "Queen Namani wrote to me every year on my birthday. But she never mentioned his identity."

"So you have no idea who he…is."

A queen's illegitimate son, sent away like a disgrace and he had risen to be the sheikh.

Suddenly, his anger, the fear in his eyes when he had thought of her marrying Zufar after learning of their child's existence—everything fell into place.

He had grown up among strangers, sent away by his mother. He had no idea who his father was. And if she had married Zufar, the entire wretched history would have been repeated with their own child.

"Adir, I'm truly sorry. But you cannot hold me responsible for something I didn't cause willingly. You didn't come back until you had decided that your revenge could have even worse consequences for Zufar."

"It matters not whether I was born a bastard out of wedlock, Amira. I would never agree for a child of mine not to know me." But it did matter because he hadn't known his parents. "It is a truth only Humera and I know."

Amir nodded automatically, her mind whirling.

So why had he come to the palace of Khalia? What had he wanted of Zufar?

Had he told her more truth than even he realized that night?

Had he come looking for family?

Would he tell her truth if she asked?

Just as she turned away from him, his fingers on her wrist pulled her back. His face was so close to hers that his breath caressed her cheek. "I will not have you play the martyr at our wedding."

She laughed. What did the insufferable man want? Even he didn't seem to know. "Believe me, Adir. I hate even aspiring to that role. Passivity has never been my favorite. Anything else Your Highness wishes to command?"

"No, you're not passive, whatever else you are." And then something almost tender glinted in his eyes. Something she wanted to burrow into. "Pick one thing. One thing, one element in this wedding will be as you want it. What do you want, Amira?"

The words hung between them as Amira stared at him with wide eyes. The arrogant tilt of his chin couldn't erase the significance of what he offered.

And suddenly, a small flicker of joy lit up in her chest.

However he coated it, this was personal. This was a small brick he had laid on the foundation of their life.

"Any chance that one element could be the

groom?" Amira taunted, hiding the longing inside of her. "I saw this young man the other day—a poet that all the women are mad about, Zara said." Adir's brows tied into a thunderous frown and she gave into the laughter bubbling up through her. "He has the most wonderful smile, I think he's the glaring one—your friend Wasim's younger brother—"

The rest of her words were swallowed up by his warm mouth. A swift, hard kiss of possession. Of utter masculine claim. A reminder that she belonged only to him. Heart thudding, Amira clung to him as he devoured her mouth.

"Do not push me, *habiba*. I already hang on a knife edge of balance."

Amira didn't misunderstand the dark glitter of desire in his eyes.

"My wedding dress… Galila and I once went shopping at this designer boutique in Abu Dhabi. This dress…it was the most gorgeous thing I'd ever seen."

"Why didn't you buy it?"

She shrugged. "My father wouldn't pay for such an expensive dress and for Zufar to pay for it, I would have had to jump through ten hoops. It was probably sold years ago but I remember the design very well. Nusrat is a dab hand at sewing and the women here, Zara says, they do such intricate work. Of course, the fabric would have to be fetched from one of the royal couture houses and we would have to pay the women because I really don't want to presume on my future—"

He nodded, pride shining in his eyes. "It will be done."

"Thank you."

On an impulse, Amira touched her mouth to his cheek. And held onto him when he would have left.

She could have left their meeting on that peaceful note.

He had granted her more than she had ever hoped from him in that small gesture about the dress. And yet something in her couldn't forget the enormity of what he had told her about his mother, couldn't stop thinking of what had brought him into her life.

"Adir…this thing with Prince Zufar…what did you ask of him?"

"That I be acknowledged as Queen Namani's son, as part of the Khalian lineage."

"What did he say?"

"He called me a dirty stain on the royal house."

And so he had not only seduced her but stolen her away on the morning of her wedding to Zufar. Amira struggled to keep her distress out of her face. Their truce was tentative, fragile. For all his kisses and generosity, she was aware of the fragile position he gave her in his life. In his personal one, at least. But she couldn't leave it alone. She couldn't shelve it when it was the basis of their entire relationship.

"It is done now, though, right? I mean, you have taken something away from Zufar, because he took something that was yours. Isn't that what you said?"

"Have I been granted my rightful place, Amira?"

And just like that, Amira's heart sank. She shook her head, no words coming to her lips.

His hand behind him, his face stony, he said, "Then no. It is not done. I will not rest until I have what is mine."

Amira sank to her bed, knowing that while everything had changed for her, nothing had changed for him in the last few weeks.

And nothing—not their child, not this wedding—would change Adir's mind.

She could not forget that. She could not forget that if she let it, Adir's inability and unwillingness to see her as anything more than a convenient wife could hurt her far more than Zufar's indifference could have done.

In fact, if she let it, it would shred her into pieces.

Their wedding day dawned with an explosion of oranges and pinks over the gorge and the valley.

Amira had bathed in a huge tub of water placed next to a roaring fire pit, her thick, long hair scented with rose attar; her skin massaged and scrubbed and polished until it gleamed golden.

On the women's side of the tent, Amira—having been attended and dressed just as elaborately as she had been on her wedding day to Zufar by no fewer than twelve women, all of whom Zara had informed her with a reverent tone considered it a privilege and honor to ready the bride of their ruling sheikh—was joined by at least twenty women, all dressed in simple, yet elegant silk dresses.

For once, she'd been grateful for Humera's authority, for the old midwife had ushered everyone out—even Zara—while Amira donned the lace petticoats that had to go under the dress. Amira didn't even question how Humera knew. The old woman knew everything.

Her slender stature meant she wasn't quite showing in cleverly cut clothes, though naked, the swell of her belly was becoming more and more noticeable.

It was something that made her nervous about her wedding night.

Amidst the colorful rugs that adorned the floor and the walls and the fluttering of bright emerald and deep reds of the women's dresses, Amira's breath had been stuck in her throat when she had been brought to the "bridal tent" as Humera had called it.

All these women and their families were so utterly loyal to Adir, so delighted to welcome

Amira into their small sphere of lives. Their respect was so automatically given because they trusted Adir's choice, because they thought she had captured their lonely sheikh's heart after all these years.

Three women played local tunes amidst laughter and a lot of oohing and aahing over each other's jewelry and clothes.

Her hands and feet had been decorated with henna in intricate swirls. Since Amira had literally run away with him with empty hands, Zara, who Amira had learned to her surprise rode the bus every day to work at Adir's IT company, had been dispatched to buy makeup from one of the luxurious high-end malls that had been built in the nearest city.

After an initial protest, Amira had given in while Zara wielded the makeup brushes with infinite delight.

Every new face that greeted her and congratulated her, every teasing glance from unmarried women like Zara and Nusrat and hushed whispers followed by a blush from one of the married women, every warm hug and genuine smile that was bestowed on her slowly released the grip of the worry that had her in its hold.

Except for Galila's friendship, which had possessed its own restrictions since Amira had been betrothed to her brother, she had been deprived of any woman's company since her mother's death.

Suddenly, it felt like she had been dropped in the middle of a warm, albeit noisy family, full of sisters and cousins and friends as she'd always hoped for. As their sheikha, she knew she couldn't share her doubts about her and Adir, but it was nice to be seen, to have the warmth that had always been lacking in her life before.

When a pregnant woman had complained about being afraid of waiting for the mobile clinic to arrive when she got close to her due date, Amira, to Humera's disapproving glance, had immediately offered to deliver the baby.

Between tears and smiles, the woman had thanked and hugged Amira and soon word spread that she was a registered obstetric nurse. It had taken a strict command from Humera asking the women not to forget that this was their future sheikha and not just any tribeswoman and that it was uncertain if their sheikh would give his wife permission to attend to the tribeswomen like a normal employee.

There had been no censure but a warning in Humera's gaze as she had looked at Amira. A gentle reminder perhaps that she had a ruthless overlord and she wasn't free to give her word in this matter.

But even Humera's warning couldn't douse her enthusiasm. There was a need here and she would do everything to see that she filled that need. This was the whole reason she had studied nursing against all odds. This was what she had envisioned her future to be in her wildest dreams.

Amira winked at one of the women who caught her gaze. If she could help out when she was needed, if she could carve a place for herself and her work amongst the tribes... For the first time in months, Amira felt hope for the future.

She could have a fulfilling life here. She would have Adir's respect, she would have her baby and she would have her work. This new life could be better than anything she'd ever hoped for.

No need for love and all the foolishness and trouble it brought.

No need to worry about keeping her emotional distance from a man who could touch her soul with one searing kiss.

Soon it was time to don her wedding dress.

A slithery gold silk—a color that was cause for celebration—with simple beading and embroidery work that the tribeswomen had toiled over during long cold nights around a huge fire pit in one of the tents that had been arranged just for the purpose.

Time to walk, flanked by all the women, toward the huge tent that had been set up with large fire pits warming it in all four corners.

Time to meet the eyes of the man waiting for her.

Dressed in traditional robes, his dark eyes rimmed with the slightest kohl, he was every forbidden dream Amira had ever had. The slight flare of his nostrils, the wicked gleam in his eyes that she was sure only she saw, told Amira what he thought of her dress. What he thought of her as she looked back at him with a suddenly bashful smile.

Right or wrong, foolish or smart, her own choices had brought her to this point in life, to this man.

And now it was truly up to her to make the best of this marriage.

She would, she promised herself fiercely. She would prove to him that she was the best thing that had happened to him. She would make their home a loving place for this child and any more they might have.

Outwardly, she bowed her head in prayer and promised obedience and love to her husband.

CHAPTER SEVEN

IT TOOK ADIR the better part of the night to extricate himself from the celebrations that continued after the wedding ceremony. He rarely, if ever, drank when he was around the encampment, respecting the elders' tradition of abstaining from alcohol, but tonight he needed a stiff drink.

Tonight, he would give anything to forget the long series of duties that rested on his shoulders, this constant…need he felt to prove himself over and over again, to the tribes, to the world. And more than anything, to himself.

It wasn't confidence he lacked. The quarterlies from his company were enough to proclaim his material wealth in his own mind.

No, it was the void he felt inside himself. A void he had felt all his life. A void that had been dug deeper and deeper by his mother's letters, instead of giving him solace.

A void that he fueled his ambition, his need for power and for something even more intangible.

At least the wedding had been a happy celebration for his own tribes and the choice of his sheikha lauded again and again.

It seemed in that matter no one could find fault with him.

Heads from four different tribes had attended the wedding, had come to give their blessing to his marriage—to openly show their support to him and maybe to thumb their nose at governments that were always trying to absorb their lands by way of some treaty or such.

His reputation and the results he had achieved with Dawab and Peshani were also constant draws. And that he had petitioned the sheikh of their neighboring country, Zyria, to enter the council of local governments had already reached certain ears.

Whether he could draw Sheikh Karim of Zyria into the council and convince him to sign the treaty that Adir had so far negotiated for two countries to sign about not encroaching the tribes' land—land that had been claimed for centuries—

was another matter. Yet every tribal chief at his table wanted to know the outcome.

Every tribal chief was vested in that outcome.

They thought Adir meant to amass more power, more connections. As a businessman, it was partly that. But he also wanted peace for the land that had reared him. He wanted to put a stop to the constant skirmishes between the countries that bordered the desert land. He wanted the tribes to thrive.

Is it a legacy that you want to create? Amira had asked him when he had explained his reason for starting the council almost a decade ago. They had been having dinner together because he had wanted to see her before he was denied the sight of her for three whole days before the wedding, according to tradition. He had wanted to lose himself in the languid heat of her mouth, to feel her lithe body in his hands before he went to his bed alone and finished himself off.

But of course, nothing was uneventful or simply relaxing when it came to Amira.

She prodded at him, poked at him until he answered. And his answers when she pushed him, he was beginning to realize, contained truths even he wasn't even aware of.

Like her perceptive question three nights ago.

Why couldn't the blasted woman just accept his answer when he had said that peace in the area was good for his business? That it invited foreign investors, that it brought money into the area—money and wealth that the tribes could really use?

But she wouldn't. When he had glared at her, she had ignored his dictates and come up with her own conclusion.

That it went beyond being a good ruler. That he wanted to make his name, that he wanted to leave a legacy.

And since he had had no good rebuttal for her infuriatingly close-to-truth conclusions, he had simply walked out on her and the dinner. Like a schoolboy who couldn't control his temper.

Why he wanted to leave a legacy had become more than evident today. It was a hard truth he still couldn't swallow.

Suddenly, the path he had set himself felt less like victory and more an eternally unreachable conclusion. When his mother had fueled his fire, had Queen Namani thought of the toll it would take on him, or what it would cost him? Had she ever considered that her words could become an unbearable burden?

Quite without a conscious decision, he had become the figurehead of the movement to keep the tribes separate from state, to preserve their way of living. So other tribes were now curious to see the impact on living and work opportunities brought by the bridges he had built between the traditionally nomadic peoples.

The chiefs of three tribes that Adir didn't rule over had a hundred questions for him. They were testing him, he knew, wondering if he truly believed in their way of life or if he was a sellout.

There had been questions about the eco-adventure tourism company he had built, loud assent when he had said that if the whole world wanted to experience the Bedouin way of life, then the tribes should at least get paid for it. They hadn't even touched the topic of oil rights in tracts of land that the tribes had lived on for several centuries.

It would mean more responsibility for him. Two other tribes ready to pick him to represent their rights when he met government officials in the neighboring countries the following year.

Except one tribal sheikh.

One tribal sheikh who had raised the question to which Adir didn't have the answer. Would never have.

And who reminded Adir that however far he came, there was something he would never have.

"You didn't come to bed."

Adir looked up from his rumination at the husky voice. His bride stood at the partition between the lounging area and the huge bed, her golden-brown hair a mass of silky tangles around her small face.

The light golden hue of the dress—so close to her own skin color that it looked like the material had been poured over her curves—had stolen his breath when she had appeared in front of him earlier that evening.

It did so again.

How had he forgotten what had been awaiting him?

The silk whispered sinuously as she moved—hovering on the edge of the space he occupied—the fabric just as expensive and lush as the wedding dress she had worn for Zufar.

But where that dress had been designed very clearly to draw attention, to advertise and court publicity, this was so simplistic in design that it showed off to perfection the beautiful woman who wore it.

More than ten women from the tribes had worked on the bodice's intricate threadwork for seven days, and Adir had seen the privilege and satisfaction in their eyes as Amira had walked in tonight.

She fought him on what she called his high-handed manner of assigning roles to her, but being a sheikha came to her naturally. Even before the wedding, she had found a way to include the women in the celebration. He had seen it during and after the ceremony—gathering people to her, getting to know them—it was in her very blood.

No training could have created that genuine interest in her eyes as she asked Humera about the tribes or one of the women about her job in his IT company. About mobile medical clinics and goat herding in the same question.

Even he hadn't realized what an absolute gem he had been stealing from Zufar. Had Zufar? Clearly not or his half brother would have treated her with more than indifference.

The dark shadows under those big eyes pricked his guilt. Was Adir doing any better, though? "I didn't realize you'd still be awake. You were weaving by the time we went in to eat."

Surprise lit up her eyes. Did she think him such a beast that he wouldn't notice his pregnant bride struggling to keep a smile but valiantly trying to greet each and every member attending the wedding? How she'd complimented the cooks who'd prepared the food; how she'd drawn her chin up and proudly answered the wife of one of the tribal chiefs about her knowledge of old traditions?

If he was a man constantly straddling tradition and progress, she was a woman who seamlessly resided in both with her education and her respect for the old. It was a remarkably complex feat that she achieved with a very simple approach—by being open and nonjudgmental of the people he ruled, whatever her personal views.

Not that she was a doormat of any kind.

All he'd heard toward the end of the celebration had been what a lovely and kind woman their sheikha was.

"I didn't wait up for you so much as I fretted over whether you would come to bed and what you would want if you came. And what I would do if you did what you want to do." Pink stole into her cheeks at this, rendering her utterly beautiful and lovely. Of course, she didn't give him a chance to interject a compliment. "Then I fretted some more over what to do if you didn't do what I thought you would do. I think I hurt my brain with a thousand thoughts running in a million directions and just fell asleep."

"Your brain must hurt a lot more frequently then," he said automatically and her face broke into a brilliant smile. That tentative quality that had remained all the last two weeks faded, the imp from their first meeting emerging. It stole his breath, which was a curiosity since his libido was already growling and nothing else should have mattered.

"May I join you, Adir?"

He didn't quite frown but couldn't manage a smile. He had a lot on his mind tonight—about his mother, about a lot of things he couldn't control and he didn't want her intruding on that. He didn't want her innocence and her probing questions. He had always dealt with this alone.

What he did want from her tonight he couldn't take, because he wouldn't be gentle. Not tonight when he was feeling this…turmoil. When he was already on edge after the uncharacteristic celibacy he had forced on himself for the last four long months.

Something he still didn't understand even now.

"I will not be much company tonight, which is what you seem to be looking for. Go back to bed."

"Will you…join me tonight?" she asked, the wariness back.

A more patient man would have taunted her back, asked if she wanted him to join her. A man who hadn't already been through an emotional whirl thanks to her unwanted, unsolicited opinions.

"Do I need to inform you of my intentions, Amira? Give you a schedule every evening as to whether I want to have marital relations or not?"

She paled. "No... I just thought we could wait—"

"No, we shall not wait to consummate this marriage. You're my wife." It was the wrong thing to say to a man whose identity had already been challenged once that night, whose very rule over the tribes was being called into question based on a fact he had no control over. "It is my wedding night, isn't it? I think I shall do as I please at the moment. If I find you're asleep when I come to bed, I will wake you to accommodate me."

He sounded like a man of a different century—a husband before women's lib. He had always considered himself an educated and enlightened man, but Amira drove him to regress to Neanderthal behavior.

She didn't flinch and yet what color had been in

her cheeks receded at his snarl. She would leave him alone now, he was sure.

And once he had gotten over his black mood, he would join her in bed and she would welcome him.

Because the one thing Amira wasn't good at was playing games. Beneath the elaborate, round-about clamor of her thoughts was plain desire. Desire that enflamed him despite his dark mood.

She wanted him next to her in that bed, above her, moving inside her. But she hadn't yet quite come to terms with her desire, nor did she know how to express it without feeling mortified. The realization that his wife needed his touch, the release he could bring, as desperately as he needed hers, went a little way to assuage his own turmoil.

But if he thought his innocent wife would retreat to lick her wounds, he was wrong. Invalidating her own question, she walked into the lounging area, as if propelled by his refusal of company. In defiance of his surly mood?

It never amazed him how much strength she possessed beneath that outward fragility.

"Even Humera avoids me when I'm in this mood," he added as a warning, unable to look away from the ravishing picture she made.

She shrugged and gracefully sank down onto the divan, on the other end. "Then Humera is fortunate. Since I'm your wife, I have no such escape route available."

"I'm giving you one."

"No, you're dictating what kind of marriage we will have. And I told you that is one place where I shall not bow to you. If you're…upset…" she looked him square in the eye, her eyes widened, and then she started again "…if you're angry and want to fume in silence, then I shall simply sit with you, in silence. Since we're married, it would be nice if you shared your thoughts with me. But if you don't want to, that is fine, too. What I will not tolerate is being completely shut out of your day just because you're in a sulky and snarly mood and then for you to visit me only when you're in the—" whatever she saw in his eyes, she licked her lower lip and Adir's blood fled south "—in the…in the mood for… sex. When I gave my promise today, I meant it.

I meant that I would share your life and I mean to share everything. Not just your bed."

Having finished her little speech, she leaned back and scooted upward on the divan. Legs tucked under her, the dress spread around her reclining form, her long neck bared to his hungry gaze, her breasts rising and falling... It was like dangling meat in front of a hungry predator.

"Are you saying I'm not allowed to touch you, Amira?" he asked, half shocked, half taunting.

Her eyes remained closed, the sweep of her lashes casting shadows against her cheekbones. "I'm saying you can have more than my body, Adir. I'm not asking you to pour out your heart. But you also don't have to protect me from your... mood swings. Believe me, I'm not going to protect you from mine."

He laughed then, a sound that rushed up from his belly, a sound that surprised himself. Even in his foul mood, she somehow made him laugh. "Mood swings and tart words...hmm. I thought I was getting a sweet-tempered wife."

"For a man who managed to unite two warring tribes, you're quite dense, aren't you? Use honey rather than vinegar if you want a sweet wife, Adir."

The minx's mouth twitched and Adir lost his hold on his control. On his hunger. "I know what to use to make you sweet, *ya habibiti*. My fingers, my mouth, my tongue."

Her breasts rose and fell rapidly. Lust came at Adir like a punch to his middle, all consuming. Suddenly, he wanted her bared to him.

Those dark pink nipples, the sharp curve of her waist, the jet black curls at the juncture of her thighs.

Sweat beaded over his forehead.

He moved toward her slowly, gently, afraid of spooking her. The tense line of her shoulders said she was aware of his proximity. But she lay there like a queen, supine, a ripe temptation.

Small beads of moisture collected on her upper lip, such plump, pink lips that they reminded him of raspberries. Tart, too.

He moved closer until his thigh touched hers, until he was leaning back beside her.

Her breaths sped up, her fingers on her stomach fluttering, like the wings of a butterfly. And suddenly, from one breath to the next, everything shifted.

She was so slender that it was barely noticeable in her normal clothes, but this close, with her reclining back, he could see the curve of her belly.

He swallowed and placed his face above hers. When she didn't jump away, even as she tensed like a taut bow, he slid his hand in under hers.

There.

Stillness came over him, all his earlier turmoil grinding to a halt.

A life they had created together.

A tiny, tiny being that he was responsible for. A child that would look to him for guidance, protection and...love.

Since he'd learned the truth, all his thoughts had been on legitimizing his child, on Amira and all the strange new things she made him feel. Fatherhood hadn't even been on his mind.

Only now did he realize what a tremendous thing had come into his life. A strange shiver gripped him.

Amira's gaze flicked open, alarm dancing in

it. She covered his hand with hers, tangling her fingers with his. "Adir? What is it?"

"Would you give up this baby for anything, Amira?"

She jerked away from him, pure aggression coiling her movements. Her glare could burn him into ashes. "How dare you even ask such a question?"

And yet the same question coiled around him, twisting and turning, choking him. "What about if I offered you the freedom you covet so much in exchange? A fresh start somewhere in the world where no man would ever rule you again? A place in a coveted university to study to your heart's content? What then?"

"No. No. No. Not for anything in this world."

A shaft of pain pinched his heart. Sharp and so incredibly real, more than anything he had ever experienced.

"Adir, you're frightening me. What…what have I done?"

He'd been an innocent babe like this when they had cast him off. His mother had professed her love in all her letters, for the man she had had to cut out of her life, for Adir. She had urged him to make something of himself. There had been an almost mad fervor to her letters in which she had poured out all the injustices done to her as she was forced to give him up and described all her festering resentment for her other children— for Zufar, Malak and even Galila.

But in the end, she had given him away. She had never tried to see him again, had forbidden him from seeing her—only directing his destiny from afar.

And as for his father... "Why is the baby so important to you? It's unexpected and...by your own admission, it ties you to a man who deceived you, yes?"

"Adir—"

"Let's not pretend that if not for the baby, you would have run away before I could catch you, Amira."

"Fine. It is important because it stemmed out of a choice I made. My very own. It grew out of a good thing."

"You still think it's a good thing that you spent the night with me even though you hate me?"

"I do not hate you. I...that night was... Let's just say, a fairy-tale night. That night and this baby are tied together now. I can't claim to love the night but hate the repercussions. How could I hate you or that night when it brought me this tiny creature?"

But unlike Amira, his mother and his father had enjoyed their affair, their love for each other—just not the result, which was him.

He took Amira's unwilling hand in his, lacing their fingers like she had done before. When he tugged her, she came, until she was sitting between his legs, her back resting against his chest, her hips grazing his thighs.

Something inside him calmed. This child of theirs she carried, this woman—they belonged to him. His own. It was atavistic, this thinking, but he couldn't help it. In a life where he had called no one his, *they* were his.

"Adir, please...tell me what brought this on. Tell me—"

"Hush, *habiba*," he said, holding her close, regretting the fact that he had scared her. It was hard to stay mad at her, he was realizing. And even worse, indifferent. "It is nothing to do with you. Or even me. The meeting with the chiefs just brought on questions."

"What kind of questions? Adir, you can't expect me to be your sheikha and not share anything of what makes you *you*."

"What is it you want to learn, Amira?"

"How did you become the sheikh? I mean, after you were sent away like that."

He buried his face in her hair, the scent of her encircling him. "When I united the Dawab and Peshani tribes, I did it unknowingly. They had been warring with each other for years, and the local governments provided just enough fuel to keep them going at each other's throats. Because as long as they were fighting—and trying to make deals to cheat each other—the oil rights on the land they occupied, vast tracts of land, was up for grabs."

Slowly, she relaxed against him. His breath stuttered when she pulled his arms around her middle, a pillow for her soft breasts. He wasn't even sure she was aware of the move. Of how she constantly tempted him, of how innately sensuous she was.

"You pointed out the obvious," she said, and he smiled.

"Yes. When I was at university in Zyria, I met an investor who saw merit in my ideas for an eco-adventure tourism company. Then from there, I went on to buy an arm of an IT company since it was clear that even the Bedouin way of living wasn't going to escape modernization completely."

"I know. I was so amazed to learn that Zara works for you."

The pride in her words made him feel a thousand feet tall—even though he'd never needed validation before. "It took Zara and me and Humera months to convince her parents that it was a good idea for her to use her brains to support the family's meager income. That they were not selling out their daughter to the modern world.

"Once we provided the bus service and they met a recruiter—another woman who works for me—they were convinced."

"And from there, everything took off." She

looked over her shoulder at him as if he had achieved the impossible. As if he were truly a hero. "You have done so much for them, Adir. You're a natural leader. Every day, I see their pride in you, their trust that you would always do the right thing for them. It is a trust you have earned."

"Today, two other tribal chiefs attended our wedding."

He could almost see her frown. "And?"

"They were testing the waters, so to speak. That the Dawab and Peshani have given up on decades of enmity is a powerful draw. That they're thriving under my leadership, finding new sources of income and livelihoods while the most traditional of them continue the old ways of goat herding has brought another tribe to be ready to grant me permission to represent them. It is a double-edged sword, a privilege to be given power to rule them. And the second chief...he questioned my birth, about my right to rule over the tribes. He asked about my parentage. About where I had sprung from. He was clearly trying to provoke me into a fight and..."

Adir would have no answer to give, Amira realized.

Even the part he knew of his parentage, he could not proclaim it to the world. He could not say he was of royal lineage, that ruling was in his bones and in his blood.

He couldn't say anything. He would have to take any insults offered him.

Suddenly, Amira wanted to call Zufar out on his pride.

And Queen Namani, what had she bred into Adir through those letters? What had she given him? Not pride, not love, whatever Adir chose to call it. But a festering resentment for his half brothers and sister.

And all this he had borne alone, until now.

"And it made you think of Queen Namani?"

"It made me think of my father, the man she had the affair with. The man she said she loved with all her heart and who in turn adored her." He ran his fingers through his hair. "Queen Namani's letters have been the driving force in my life for as long as I remember."

Curiosity about the old queen ate through

Amira. She couldn't even believe it was the same woman that had been her best friend's temperamental mother. "When did she send them?"

"One letter every birthday." The monotony of his voice tore at her for it completely belied the emotion in his eyes. "By the time I began to understand who she was to me, I waited for that day every year. It was a prize, a gift."

"What…what were those letters about?"

"A piece of her heart, just for me, she said. Her true legacy, she called me. She urged me to study, to take control of my life, every letter on every birthday reminding me that I was destined for great things. That I was not to neglect my education at any cost. That I was to rise through the world. That I was not to grow weak in the face of any hurdle. That my path would always be that of a loner, if I wanted to reach my true destiny. Not to trust anyone, not to give into the whims of my heart. That I was to make an advantageous match with a powerful bride when it was time to wed."

The path of a loner… Destiny before heart… *Ya Allah*, was it any wonder he was so remote, so isolated from everyone? The rage Amira felt for the dead queen choked her.

She swallowed it away, for she didn't want to disturb the small intimacy. "Did you tell her that you achieved even more than she could predict? That you had been chosen to rule the tribes?"

"No."

Amira's heart ached for the pain contained in that single word. She forced herself not to look at him for the fear of seeing that pain in his eyes. Because if she did, then she wouldn't be able to control the outrage that filled her. She couldn't arrest the words that needed to be said. "Why... why not?"

"The condition of receiving her letters was that I was never to contact her. Never to betray her confidence. Never to let another soul learn who she was to me."

"But you went to see them after her funeral."

"On her orders. She urged me to claim my place in that last letter."

After there was no harm to her own reputation. When she was no longer in this world to deal with her mistakes. What a coward Queen Namani had been!

"When the old sheikh told me he had chosen me as his successor, it was her words that filled me with confidence. I never gave the identity of my father another thought...until today."

"And today, that man made you wonder about your father. About what kind of a man would not even look up the child he had fathered on the woman he supposedly adored and loved. About the woman who gave you a dream, lured you with it but kept it out of your reach. A woman who only bred anger toward—"

He jerked her up so fast that she would have fallen off the divan if it weren't for his tight grip. "She was forced to give me up. Queen Namani loved me."

"And yet you asked me if I would give this baby up for anything. I wouldn't, Adir. Even if I could understand how she had to, I don't understand her. With Zufar and Galila, she—"

"Enough, Amira! You, with your naive outlook of the world and your loyalty still tied to Zufar, you wouldn't understand. She loved my father and she hated parting with me. I will not hear a word about this from you, ever again. Do you understand?"

Amira wanted to say no, but that she was finally beginning to understand him.

To understand the hold Queen Namani's words still had over him.

She was a perfect woman in his mind—his mother who had spurred him on and on to better things in life. Filled his mind with useless words about destiny and loneliness. And who had made him blind to everything else.

She wanted to argue that the queen had done him more harm than good. She wanted to tell him what she knew of Galila's childhood and how uncaring and neglectful she had been of Zufar, Malak and Galila.

That Zufar, who represented everything Adir did not have, for all his legitimacy hadn't even had what Adir had received from their mother. That Adir's arrival, the knowledge of the letters she had written him, would have been punishment enough to all three of his siblings.

But she could say none of it.

Because Adir was not prepared to hear her.

He wouldn't see the truth. Maybe Queen Namani had truly loved this son she'd been forced to give up, had been weak and selfish, and he had become an outlet for her to thumb her nose at her husband and even her other children.

He wouldn't see that he had become a silent rebellion for a weak woman.

The very thought made Amira want to growl in pain. That she had cast this honorable man in such hard words made her want to rage.

Queen Namani had not only given him up, but also used him for her own agenda.

He would never be prepared to hear the truth. He would never realize that, for all he was in the dark about his father's identity, he didn't need it.

Adir Al-Zabah was a man to be reckoned with, a natural leader, a born king.

This husband of hers, who was noble and thought of his tribes and their needs, was still haunted by a past he couldn't fix. And he couldn't see that Queen Namani had stolen more from him than he could ever imagine—the chance of having a relationship with his siblings, the chance to let the past be left in the past.

The chance of ever inviting more into his life.

And while he was mired in the complex truths of the past, while he was still under the hold of his mother's ghost, there would be room for nothing else in his life.

Or his heart.

It would only ever be a marriage of convenience.

He would only ever be her husband by law. He could never own a place in her heart. He could never hurt her, for she knew what not to expect from him.

And the strange realization gave her the courage to give comfort. The guts to simply offer what he needed from her tonight.

She offered the only thing she knew he would allow her to do. Her legs shook as she let her body sway toward him, giving herself over.

She went to her knees between his thighs, her own need drowning out other cries. His fingers manacled her wrists, his anger vibrating in the air around them.

Amber eyes darkened to a burnished copper, his mouth set into a flat uncompromising line, he held her gaze.

Breath punched up through her throat as her breasts pressed against his hard chest, her soft belly sinking against his abdomen, the press of his arousal a brand against her skin.

"I'm sorry," she said, leaning her forehead against his. "You're right. I don't understand. I can't imagine the…frustration you must feel. I can't imagine the strength it takes for you to be who you are."

She pressed her lips to his and whispered her apology. Again and again. Between soft kisses and hurried breaths. Between the raspy purr of her lips against his and the enticing swirl of her tongue inviting him.

She couldn't bear it if he told her it meant nothing to him except that it would ensure her obedience. If he said it was his due in that arrogant way of his.

If he said she was weak for still living in her naive world.

She still had a life with him, with their baby.

She had a family of her own—the three of them and more, in the coming years. She had a taste of his reluctant respect, she had his name and she had his desire. That had to be enough.

That would be enough.

She clasped his cheeks, the bristle of his beard rasping against her palms in sensuous torture. His nostrils flared, his hips pressing roughly against hers, even as he sought to control his anger. And his lust. This relentless need she could see in his eyes. Because it was the same for her.

Another wet, warm kiss against his mouth, the scent of him coiling lazily in her limbs. She dragged the tips of her teeth against his hard jaw. Felt the reward of his fingers roughly tangling in her hair.

She thrust her tongue into his unwilling mouth when he growled. Stroked it against his tongue, like he had done to her just a few days ago. The length and breadth of her pressed into him, she made love to his mouth with hers, willing his control to shatter. Willing him to take over.

And when, with a growl that reverberated up

through his chest, he claimed ownership of the kiss, she shivered all over. In relief, in desire.

When he thrust his tongue into her mouth roughly, hungrily, she welcomed him. She welcomed the tips of his fingers digging into her hips, she reveled in how his chest crushed her sensitive breasts. She gloried in the evidence of his hard arousal against her lower belly, in the molten warmth he created at her sex.

His fingers crawled into her hair, pulling and tugging at the pins in it until it fell to her waist. She moaned loudly when he sank his fingers into the thick mass and pulled her closer.

Possessive and rough, his control was in shreds at her feet. He was shaking with desire and Amira answered in kind. Answered with the only truth he would allow between them.

"I'm glad I met you, Adir. I'm glad you're my husband, that you will be the father to my child. I'm so glad that I chose you that night. And I would gladly do so again and again, given half the chance."

CHAPTER EIGHT

I'M SO GLAD that I chose you that night. And I would gladly do so again and again.

How did such an innocent know what words to say to ensnare such a jaded man as him? To push him to the edge of his control?

How could one surrender and gain victory at the same time? Her words and her eyes, her kisses lit a fire in Adir's blood.

He took her mouth with a feral hunger he could not corral into submission. She melted under his kiss, her lips so sweet yet incinerating, her moans soft but packing a punch, her strokes to keep up with him so inexperienced and yet filled with a ferocious desire that matched his own.

Hands on her back, he crushed her to him while he groped for the zipper of the dress, like a teenage boy touching his first woman. She threw her head back, baring her neck to him—another invitation he could not resist. Her pulse thrummed violently at her neck, the scent of her rose perfume emanating from her soft skin.

While he tugged the hidden zipper down with one hand, he scored the long line of her neck with his teeth. He dug his teeth in at her pulse point and suckled that skin into his mouth, eager for the taste of her to sink into his very marrow.

She tasted of sweat and sweetness, an incredibly erotic combination that only made him hunger for more.

"I will taste you everywhere tonight, *ya habibi*," he promised, his voice gone so deep and husky that even he barely recognized it. That night, he had barely had the time to indulge himself, hardly any time to explore the heady explosion her body promised. "I will lick your flesh, sink my teeth in wherever I please. I will taste the honey between your legs and you will fracture from the unbearable pleasure of it."

He did so, hard and deep, until her pale golden skin bore his mark, like a savage from centuries ago. Lust pounded in his blood as her skin instantly bruised.

She jerked closer to him, her knees trembling,

her breath a rough accompaniment to his caresses.

A sob broke out of her as he softly licked the bruise he had given her. When she thrashed against him, searching for more, eager for more, he gave it to her by rocking into the cradle of her thighs. Pressing his erection against the warmth he knew was waiting for him.

She let out another sob as she flung her arms around his shoulders and clung to him.

For every action, there was an equal and opposite reaction—she was Newton's law embodied. He smiled, making a note to tell her of his idiotic comparison. His smart wife would surely get a kick out of that.

"Adir, please… I want more. This dress…it rubs and caresses…"

"Then we will rip it off, *ya habibi*." He grabbed the neckline in his hands when she jerked back from him, her arms protectively held against the bodice of the gown. He had forgotten that he had undone the zipper. A pale golden shoulder peeked at him as the bodice loosened. And the upper curve of one breast was a tantalizing reminder of what awaited him.

Cheeks pink with color, hair a glorious mess around her face, lips swollen with his rough kisses—she was a wet dream come true. A complex, blood-pounding combination of innocence and sensuality.

"No." She settled the fabric over her chest with her palm in a loving caress. Unwittingly making her nipples poke against the slithery silk.

Adir groaned and rubbed his hand against his face. "Come back to me, Amira."

She shook her head, making the long locks cover her face. "I…" She licked her lips and flinched with pain at the indent he had left on her lower lip with his teeth. Instead of feeling guilty for hurting her, lust swirled through him, demanding more. "I will not let you tear this dress. My wedding dress… It's a symbol of so many things to me, so many good things, it's precious to me. I mean to keep it for decades to come."

Decades to come. It was a vow spoken between them, a promise given freely in a relationship he had forced on her.

The rightness of her words soothed a place he didn't realize needed soothing, filled a void he hadn't known existed within him.

He didn't tell her he had no intention of tearing something that was clearly so important to her. Instead, he raised a brow, as if considering her request. For all her innocence and surrender, his wife had a backbone of steel. If she thought he was ordering her around, she would take back that surrender.

And he needed it right now more than he needed air.

"Then you may take it off and put it away."

The fire pit hissed in the silence, while outside the tents, the soft tinkle of instruments permeated the air. They were still celebrating his union with this enchantress. He was a fool to have wasted so many hours roiling in that chief's comments when he should have been here with her.

Enjoying this.

"Take it off? Here?" she asked softly, finally, taking in the light from the solar lanterns around them. Since he hadn't been disturbing her sleep, he hadn't turned any of them down.

A golden glow filled the room, the colorful rugs and throws reflecting a kaleidoscope of colors and shapes onto her form.

Not an inch of her would be hidden from his sight, a realization she seemed to come to at the same moment, for she frowned and looked around again. Her wide eyes filled her face, her cheeks flushing with color.

"But don't you want to go back there?" She pointed behind her to where his vast bed awaited, shrouded in darkness. Another fire pit and the fur rugs provided warmth there.

"No, not today. Some other time, some other night, I will come to that bed, find you in the darkness and be inside you while you slowly surface from sleep, while you're still dreaming of me. Today, I want you here."

Swallowing nervously, she looked at the thin walls reflecting their silhouettes.

"No one would dare wander close to our tent, *ya habibiti*. Nor dare even to glance at even their sheikha's shadow. The night will not carry any of the sounds we make. Now take off that dress and return to me, before I lose the little patience I'm struggling to keep. Come here, Amira," he said, patting the space between his thighs. Slowly, he relaxed into his stance.

Her doe-like gaze went to the place on the divan he pointed to and then to his throbbing erection—pressing upward and blatantly clear against the soft fabric of his robes.

If she stared at him any harder... He laughed, his balls becoming tighter. His blood pounded with such savage hunger that he wondered if he should even be touching her right then. But he let that concern him only for a second longer. The idea of not being inside her within the next few breaths was unendurable.

She would take him and he would ensure she was sobbing with pleasure by the end of it.

"Look at me," he commanded and she obediently did. More out of curiosity than true obedience, he had no doubt. Slowly, he reached for the hem of his robes and pulled them up and over his head.

Leaving himself utterly naked to her roving gaze.

She gasped, a soft, feminine sound that he

wanted to hear again and again, and much more loudly. She had made that sound when he had thrust into her—a cross between pain and pleasure, a gasp of wonder.

He needed that in his ears again, he needed her warm breath fluttering the hair on his chest, he needed the silky slide of her thighs against his hair-roughened ones. He needed the soft cries she emitted when he moved inside her, the low keening sound she made in her throat when she climaxed.

He got harder and longer as she studied that part of him, her teeth digging into her lower lip.

"Oh... I... I don't remember you being that... big." Again, a lick of her lower lip. A nervous swallow. But she didn't shy away from studying him greedily. She didn't even do it covertly. No, she looked at him boldly, possessively. "You will hurt me."

"Not today, not ever again. You're a nurse, remember your studies, Amira. You were a virgin last time. The queen's famed gardens are not the most conducive place to making a woman's first time great and—"

"It *was* great. It was…" She closed her eyes and swayed and the bodice of her dress slipped a little further, showing him the thin strap of her slip. A bold red strap.

His blood heated a little more. But he waited and watched, the thrust of her breasts, the small smile playing around her lips a reward in itself.

"So good." She opened her eyes and a fierce blush moved up her chest and neck to her cheeks. "I touched myself after…a few times. Between my legs," she clarified, as if he couldn't understand. As if he wasn't stopping himself from pouncing on her by the skin of her teeth.

The image of her touching herself, her fingers delving between those folds, the wetness that had soaked his fingers that night coating her own, the bundle of nerves at the top throbbing for his touch…

"And?" A word that reverberated with rough need.

"And it was not the same. I… I was able to arouse myself… I closed my eyes and thought of you…your weight on me, your hard thighs, the muscles in your back flexing under my touch, the way you moved in and out... I couldn't breathe for wanting you back inside me again, but whatever I did with my fingers, it was not enough. I could not...bring myself to..." and then, in front of his eyes, his shy wife transformed into something else, owned her desire "...to orgasm." She paused. "I... I shouldn't have told you that. I don't want you to think..." Dismay filled her eyes. "Your opinion means a lot to me, Adir."

And just like that, she unmanned him by her candor, by her open vulnerability. In this, he would give her honesty, too. He had the ability to, at least. "You've no idea how arousing it is to know that you get wet just by thinking of me. Knowing that I can bring you to that edge of desire. But what I would not ever tolerate is you thinking of another man like that. Is that understood?"

"Yes. Will you promise not to think of another woman moving forward, too, Adir? I feel such rage if I even think of you touching another woman, looking at another woman."

"You're all I want, *ya habibiti*. For four months, you're all I've thought of as I've brought myself to release. And tonight, it will be pleasure unlike you've ever known before."

"Even more than that night?"

He smiled wickedly, loving that much about her. Her curiosity, her innate zest for more out of life would always win over any other fear, any atrocities she had been dealt. "Yes, much, much more," he promised fiercely.

She nodded, and the line that tied her brows cleared. Slowly, holding his gaze, with utter care for the damned garment, she pushed it off her shoulders and chest.

The soft red...thing she wore underneath was silky, flimsy and so provocative as it bared half her breasts. Which he realized, with an utterly masculine satisfaction, were already fuller and lusher.

The low V neckline barely skated the line over her nipples.

Adir's breath caught in his throat as she wiggled her hips to let the dress pool down at her feet. There was a flash of a sleek thigh as she stepped over the dress. The black lace hem ended miles above her knees, baring all of her toned thighs and barely, just barely hiding her sex from his sight.

She turned and picked up the dress gently, and in the process flashed her buttocks at him. Adir smiled, wondering if he should tell her what he was sure was inadvertent.

The sight of her bare bottom while she bent over the dress... He wanted to crawl to her, push her head down to the rug and bury himself inside her, to take her like that. He was almost off the divan before he countered the urge.

Not tonight. His wife was adventurous, yes, but one step at a time.

Another time, he promised himself, when her belly was big with his child and he could not cover her body like he could now. Then he would take her from behind, in that utterly dominating position, and yet he would have to be gentle, for he could no more bear the thought of hurting her than he could bear the thought of walking away from the desert—the only home he had ever known.

The challenge it would be to his base instincts, the anticipation of it made his blood sing.

As if intent on torturing him, she straightened the dress and let it hang over a reclining chair. And only then did she turn toward him.

He had no idea what she saw in his face but she let out a long exhale. As if to brace herself. Her eyes full of a vulnerability that pierced him, she placed a hand on her belly, as if she could find support from the silk, and asked, "Do you like it? Remember the day you got so angry that I went with Zara and a couple of other women to that luxury mall? Wasim turned red and ran so fast when he saw Zara and me stop in front of the lingerie store. I told him he shouldn't follow us so closely but he wouldn't listen."

"If I had known what you'd had in mind, I would have taken you myself. And your safety is never a thing to be taken lightly, Amira. Promise me you acknowledge that."

"I do," she said so earnestly that he knew he didn't have to worry that she would take foolish risks. He kept forgetting what a levelheaded woman she was for her age. "I didn't ask you because I wanted it to be a surprise. There are certain things that should remain secret between a husband and wife. Even Humera agrees."

He scowled, knowing that she was once again testing the waters between them. Seeing how far she could push him before he pushed back. "In matters of lingerie, keep your secrets, Amira. But only there."

"Only there," she agreed, and then slowly she came to him.

Adir moved to the edge of the divan, until she was standing between his thighs, her breasts near his face.

It wasn't going to work this way. Not in this state. He would hurt her if he didn't find release first. And that was unacceptable.

And even as lust rode him hard, and the need for release clamored in his blood, Adir knew that she had sneaked under his skin. That something inside him was already changing, morphing and reforming to include this woman. That slowly but surely Amira herself was sinking into his blood.

And for a man who had not known love except in words written by a lonely woman years ago, for a man who had conquered the desert and the harsh challenges it presented, the prospect was utterly daunting.

And totally out of his control.

His skin was like hot velvet, rough but smooth at the same time. And the glide of it against her bare skin, the rough rasp of his thighs against her soft ones…they both groaned at that first skin-to-skin contact.

Her nipples, even through the flimsy silk, pebbled against his chest. And his erection…oh, God, it was fire and heat and steel pressing into her soft belly.

Sensations overwhelmed her, clamoring for her attention, and Amira closed her eyes, welcoming the onslaught. His fingers were callused, rough against her soft skin. The bruise he had given her at her neck pulsed, a perfect contrast of pain that made the pleasure coursing through her that much more powerful, that much sharper.

She sank her fingers into his hair, took a deep breath of that masculine scent. He felt like heaven. Like a safe haven. Like an exhilarating place to land.

"You're like pure silk," he said, puncturing the words with a harsh curse she didn't even understand.

He gave her no warning. By word or the flicker of an eyelid.

She gasped as he grabbed the edges of the neckline and pulled until it tore with a loud rasp. Spine arching, she clutched his head as he took her nipple into his mouth.

Teeth and tongue and wet warmth, there was nothing he didn't do to that aching bud.

Raw heat broke over her skin. His tongue licked at the needy tip, flicked at it again and again. When Amira pressed her fingers into his head, he laughed—a faint, wicked sound he buried in her skin before opening his mouth wide and closing it over her breast again.

This time, he did what she was urging him, what she was begging him to do. He suckled with deep, hard pulls. She jerked as wetness rushed over her sex, coating her thighs in a way that felt so wanton, so utterly wicked. Cupping one, he moved his mouth to the other breast, licking a wet path across and causing aching pulls in counter rhythm to his caress as he kissed her.

She rubbed her thighs shamelessly, the wetness between only intensifying the need for pressure.

Amira gasped and sobbed. Needing him inside her so desperately. "Please, Adir, inside me, now."

"No. Not yet… Four months is too long, *habiba*. I'm sorry, Amira, I'm sorry."

She had no idea what he was apologizing for and she didn't care.

He would never hurt her, not willingly, she knew that now. And she would follow him anywhere under the desert sun.

"Whatever you will give, Adir, please hurry. I feel…empty without you inside me."

He groaned, his movements becoming urgent, rough.

His hands moved from her shoulders to her waist and then further down below, to the hem of her negligee. A harsh growl erupted from his mouth, pinging over her nerves as his palms discovered her bare bottom.

"No panties?" he whispered against her wet

nipple, followed by a catlike flick over the turgid tip.

"No…the saleswoman assured me it didn't require…"

Her words misted away as he bunched the gown and pulled it up behind her, until her sex was bared to him. She longed for his fingers, his hardness there. She was vibrating with such need, she was ready to take him in hand and push him inside her.

But of course, the beast had other plans. He took her fingers and wrapped them around his hardness. "Stroke me," he commanded with such dark desire that Amira forgot all about her own body's demands. His forehead resting in the valley between her breasts, he seemed to fight his harsh breathing.

Such fervor, such need clamored in those amber eyes that she would have done anything he asked of her to satisfy that need. To be the one who pushed him to the edge. To be the one he shattered for.

"Show me how," she begged. "I want to please you. Show me how to do it right, Adir." Now the command was in her tone. She felt as if she would break if she wasn't the one that brought him the release she could see him craving.

Why was he fighting this? Didn't he know she was putty in his hands?

"If I do," he breathed against her skin, with a self-deprecating smile, "if I put my hand over your soft one and make you grip me, stroke me the way I need it, I will come instantly." She blushed at his blunt language, even as she boldly explored him with her fingers. "Four months is a long time for a man to be celibate. But if I move inside you, it will be too…short."

"You haven't been with anyone," she said, feeling a surge of something in her chest she couldn't even name.

"No."

Just that. One word. No explanation. No concession.

Adir in his true form.

She licked her lips and with a groan, he took her mouth in a hard, swift kiss. "If you find…if you come in my hands," she said, refusing to use euphemisms anymore with him, and was reward by his wicked smile, "how long before you will be able to do it again?"

This time, his raucous laughter, she was sure, could be heard all through the encampment. Tight grooves formed in his cheeks and his sweat-sleek chest shook against hers. "Selfish little thing, aren't you?"

She shrugged. "Just making sure you have a little…stamina left for me." She did a put-upon, troubled sigh, fighting the utter joy that wanted to bubble up in laughter. "You know, marriage is all about compromises and a little give-and-take."

When he kissed her again, it was soft, slow, almost reverent. As if he didn't know what to do with her. The expression in his eyes took her breath away. He wasn't a man given to words, she was realizing, but he felt something for her.

Perhaps just a little spark but it was there.

"It will be slow and deep and I can take my time inside you. I would reward you in return multiple times."

"Now you're speaking in my language."

No sooner had she said the words than he wrapped his fingers over hers. She pumped her grip up and down as he showed her. Again and again, while the soft head rubbed and pushed against her belly. While one rough hand cupped one breast, and one cupped her buttock and he took unapologetically what he needed from her.

Just from her. Only her.

Amira wouldn't have closed her eyes if her life had depended on it.

Those penetrating amber eyes closed, he thrust his hips up and forward in a counter rhythm while she worked her fist up and down, his breath shallow and fast, his skin gleaming with sweat, his neck and shoulder muscles corded so tight— he looked as if he was hewn from the rocks that lay over the gorge. It was a sight Amira would never forget.

His thrusts became faster, the angles and grooves of his face harsher, deeper and then he gave a guttural cry against her breast, before he was shuddering in her arms.

And his release coated her belly.

Amira stared in a sort of rapturous wonder. How could his release give her such satisfaction? Why did seeing him in that moment give him such a hint of vulnerability when he was truly anything but?

The intimacy of the moment, the way he held her as he broke apart… Amira felt as if she had been reformed in his passion.

In that moment, he was hers. Just a little. Only hers.

Not the sheikh of warring tribes. Not a corporate businessman. Not Queen Namani's discarded son. Or Zufar's resented half brother.

He was just her husband, the man she loved with all her heart.

She pushed sweat-streaked hair from his forehead and pressed a tender kiss to his temple. "Is this how it feels when you bring me to release?"

He looked up and that hint of vulnerability—she hadn't imagined it—disappeared when he smiled that masculine, arrogantly devilish smile that melted her heart just a little.

If they had a boy, she hoped he had that smile of his father's. That glimpse of rakishness that Adir wore beneath the mantle of duty and responsibility. That love of the harsh desert land and all its people.

"It feels like I'm on top of the world when you moan through your release, when you fall apart around my fingers. It feels like..." hands on her buttocks, he lifted her, leaving her no choice but to straddle his hips and then before she could blink, he was gliding into her on a smooth stroke, and Amira clung to his shoulders, the velvet heat of him inside sending a rough, guttural sound up through her throat "...I can conquer anything. Have I risen enough to satisfy my sheikha?"

"Oh..." No words came to her for he had impaled her so thoroughly. "It feels too much this way. Like you're..."

He instantly frowned. "Does it hurt?"

When his hands moved to her hips to pull her off, she fought his grip and pushed down. "No, Adir, please don't leave me."

The slide of her body over his made them both groan together.

"I won't." Tenderly, he pushed the hair off her forehead now. His mouth when it met hers was soft, warm, a melding of more than just bodies. He kissed her as if she were precious to him, as if he couldn't bear to part with her. As if his kisses could say things he couldn't himself. "Relax, *habiba*. Listen to your body."

She took a deep inhale and tried the up-and-down motion again. Another groan fell from her mouth, pleasure fluttering awake in her lower belly.

In knots and waves, it inched into her limbs, as if she were made of drugged honey.

"Now?" he asked.

She smiled and arched her spine. The movement sent her breasts rubbing against his chest and a hiss of male pleasure rent the air.

"Now it feels like heaven."

He moved back on the divan until her knees were on either side of his hips, until he was embedded so deeply within her that Amira couldn't breathe for the tight friction of him inside her walls.

She ran her hands all over him—the jutting tautness of his shoulders, his sweat-slicked back, the ropes of lean muscles across his chest, scraping her fingers over flat, brown nipples.

And he submitted to her touch, as if it were her due. And she loved him all the more for it.

"Now, shall I teach you how to touch yourself just as I taught you to touch me?"

Eyes wide, cheeks full of heat, she stared at him. "You want me to touch myself?"

A deliciously wicked smile split his mouth. "Just when I'm there to enjoy it, yes."

She returned his wicked smile but with an added thoughtful smirk. "And you? Will you only…pleasure yourself when I'm around?"

He laughed and the sound was even more arousing than feeling him inside her. "I'm hoping I don't have to since now you're here to do it for me. And before you argue the same point, in this position—" he thrust up as though to remind her "—it would work better."

When she nodded, he took her hand and brought it between their bodies. Heat broke out over every inch of her skin as he guided her fingers to the exact spot where she'd ached for him.

Her spine arched again as he flicked at that sensitive place with his finger. "Keep doing that when I thrust up."

More than happy to be his pupil, Amira shed the last layer of her inhibitions. His honed torso leaning back, he thrust up into her tight heat while watching her fingers move over her clitoris with hooded eyes.

"Move, Amira, as you want to."

That ache was already building in her lower body, deep waves radiating out when he thrust up and she rubbed herself.

Hand on his shoulder, Amira let herself go. Their bodies soon found a rhythm and, as if he knew her body and needs better than she did herself, he increased the pace.

Soon, Amira didn't know if she was earthbound or flying. Her breasts bounced up and down as she undulated over him. When he cupped one and brought it to his mouth just as his body pounded up into her, she fragmented.

His name fell from her lips like a keening cry as bliss suffused her every breath, every limb and joy filled her heart.

He picked her up, while he was still inside her, and brought her to his bed. Hands raising her bottom, he glided in and out of her, in deep, short thrusts.

His own quick release followed soon after and

again Amira witnessed the pleasure it wrought on his face, the way he held her when they were both sweat-slicked and the scent of sex permeated the air.

When he rubbed her lower lip with the pad of his thumb as if he couldn't let her go just yet.

When he grabbed a towel from somewhere and gently wiped her between her legs as if he had done it a thousand times and would for thousands more nights to come.

When he pressed a gentle, soft kiss to her cheek and brought her closer to his body. When his palm, as always, settled on her belly and he asked if she was okay.

She was okay. More okay than she had ever been in her life.

Because, for the first time in her life, she felt like she was home. She was where she belonged.

CHAPTER NINE

TWO WEEKS INTO being married, Adir wondered why he had waited so long to take on a wife. Like Humera and Zara and Wasim—who had become Amira's biggest champions—kept reminding him, it was Amira that made the institution so agreeable.

Apparently, there wasn't a single man or woman in the camp that didn't adore his wife.

Adir couldn't quite find a fault with her, either—not that he'd been looking for one. In two weeks, their desire for each other had only grown and whatever he asked her to do—or whatever he desired to do to her—his wife jumped in with both feet.

The only niggles in his perfect marriage were their constant fights about her health and the one topic he had forbidden her from bringing up—Queen Namani and her other children.

More than once, he had seen the struggle in

her eyes—something she wanted to say when he mentioned a letter from his mother or his past. Since everything concerned with his past or his formative years seemed to lead to Queen Namani or the letters, he had forbidden her to ask questions about his past or even mention it.

Dismay filling her eyes, she had said, "We will never move forward with our life if we don't face your past together."

He didn't agree with it. They had a perfect life together and talking about his dead mother or her other children wasn't going to make it better.

When it came to Amira's health, on the other hand, Adir knew he was being irrational. At least partly.

For every tenet he laid down about her resting during the hot days, her sleep, her food that she only picked at, his wife defied him. She called him a brute, a beast, her jailer, for after learning that she had fainted of heat stroke when she had been visiting Zara, he had forbidden her to leave their tent at all.

He had even broached the topic of sending her

away to his residence in the city. But the stubborn woman refused to leave him.

"I plan to have at least three to four children, and what will you do? Send me away and confine me completely for the next decade? Live separately?" Eyes shining with unshed tears, arms locked tight around his waist, she had burrowed into him one evening.

Having never been the recipient of such frequent physical affection—it never struck him to touch her outside bed except when he kissed her—he had stiffened. But even more shocking had been her matter-of-fact statement about having three to four children. Stunned was an understatement of his own reaction.

He had unhooked her arms from around him, trying to wrap his brain around the fact. "Three to four children?"

"Yes. I hated being an only child. And I want a big family." Then she had sobered, noticing his lack of reaction. Or maybe his shock. "Don't you want more than this child?"

"I...haven't thought that far ahead."

"But you want to be a father, yes? We didn't plan this child, but—"

"Of course, I want to be a father. But I would prefer to do the planning of our lives. Not be informed of your own plans."

She had glared at him, the only one who ever dared to do so with such impunity. "And what is my part in all this? To be a willing vessel when you decide you're ready to impregnate me again? I'm not your subject, Adir. I'm your wife."

"And as my wife, you'll obey me. As to four children, I will think about it."

And then of course she had said the one thing he didn't want to hear. "Imagine how different your life would have been if you had grown up with Zufar and Malak and Galila, if you had—"

To which he had walked out with no response.

He hadn't gone back to their tent that evening, choosing to spend it with the Dawab since he'd been visiting them anyway.

But what he'd been doing was avoiding her. Avoiding the same discussion she was hell-bent on having even as he forbade her again.

His stubborn wife was like a dog with a bit in

her teeth. Forever bringing up the subject of the queen and her other children. Forever planting doubts in his mind.

Sharing your day with me, your life with me, hasn't made any less of a ruler out of you, has it? They like seeing you happy. They want to see you happy. The queen was wrong in making you think you had to do this alone. I wish you would let me share what I know of them. Of her.

She poked at him relentlessly, to what end he had no idea.

Of course, the idea of growing up with his mother was never far away from his thoughts. Did she think he didn't wonder what it felt like to be with family? To know one's own roots? To share happiness and grief alike with siblings?

But he had never been given the choice. He'd been denied everything that was his due. And when he had asked for it, when he had demanded it, Zufar had called him a dirty stain.

The only thing that had sustained Adir growing up were those letters. But the only person he had ever been able to count on was himself.

No one else.

He had never received anything that he hadn't worked for in life, anything he hadn't planned and achieved himself, and every time Amira got close to him, every time he spied the something he couldn't define in her eyes, it made him want to run far and fast.

It made him want to shut her down.

It made him hurt her. Even when he had promised himself he wouldn't.

And since he had had no solution, he had stayed away.

When he had returned late the previous night, after having been gone for two days, she had been so silent, almost a shadow of herself. When he'd demanded that she be her normal self, she had smiled a brittle smile that made his chest ache.

"Is this what you mean to do? Punish me when I disagree with you by simply leaving me alone for as long as you please? And then returning to command me to be happy and smiling? Demand that I welcome you into my body, too?"

He had had no answer for her except to say that he had had not a single relationship where there were so many expectations on him. Where he was given things he hadn't earned or asked for, like her trust and affection, and he didn't know how to reciprocate.

At twenty-one, he had become the sheikh and that was the role he always played. No one to question him when he was wrong. No one to demand his time or attention.

And since he had known he was in the wrong and he couldn't bear to see that spirit of her bent, much less broken, he had apologized and carried her back to their bed.

It was the first night he had not made love to her. Because as much as he'd been aching to be inside her, he hadn't wanted her to be right. He didn't want to be the man who shut his wife down emotionally but took physical release. As if she were nothing but a conduit.

He wanted to be more to her, he wanted more out of their relationship, but he had no idea how. It was as if there was a wall between him and the rest of the world, a world that had been erected, brick by brick, by his mother's words.

Was Amira right? Had his mother been selfish?

And then he had hated himself for doubting her.

And so, he had just held Amira in his arms while she had clung to him.

Now, as the pink seeping through under the tents said it was dawn, he woke her up with soft kisses. Having woken up fully aroused again, his erection neatly nestled against her soft buttocks as she burrowed into him in search of warmth, he laid a line of soft kisses against the arch of her spine.

Despite his common sense warning him that his fragile wife needed rest, he couldn't help himself. But he had barely rubbed his fingers over those plump nipples and slowly parted her folds to see if she was wet, than with a grumble, she asked him what he was doing.

The deep shadows under her eyes—worse than the past week—chastened him enough. He pulled both his hands to himself, said sorry and asked her to rest.

To which his oh-so-biddable wife said she couldn't go back to sleep now that he had so thoroughly aroused her. And did he mean to step out and leave her to finish herself with her own fingers so that she could go back to sleep?

"Amira, I need you," he whispered, as close to an admission as he could ever come to.

And his generous wife turned to him, her sleep-mussed eyes glowing with affection. With tenderness. "I would never deny you, Adir. I didn't last night, either."

"I know," he whispered, while kissing every inch of her body. He said sorry again and again, for things he couldn't give. For things he didn't want to give her.

He smiled into her hair—a deep vein of fulfillment spreading through his entire body as he thrust lazily into her tight heat.

Even now, while her climax claimed her and her inner muscles clamped and released him with such mind-numbing, spine-tingling rhythm that his own release tingled up through the backs of his thighs and sent pleasure splintering through him, he didn't know how the witch had manipulated him into doing what he hadn't meant to.

His breath burning through his lungs as if he had run a marathon, he pulled her back to rest against his chest. Like a magnet turning to true north, his palm found the slight swell of her belly and settled there.

"Amira, are we…is everything okay?" he whispered at her ear, combing through the long, silky hair.

When she didn't answer, he turned her onto her back. Cheeks full of color, she would hardly look at him.

His heart threatened to burst out of his chest. Out of fear or happiness, he had no idea. It was a sensation he had never encountered before.

"Amira, what is it? Are you sore? Does it hurt?"

Sleep-mussed eyes stared back at him with such longing that he flinched and sat up. He didn't want to see such naked affection in her eyes. He could not reciprocate it and Amira was fragile enough to be crushed by this.

Already he had made a mess of their first fight. Already he had hurt her with his inability to communicate. He didn't know how to have a relationship where so much was asked of him. No parent, no sibling, no friend had ever been a part of his life.

If he commanded something as sheikh, it was done without question. Even Humera, for all she had raised him, had become distant in the past decade, for she very clearly believed in the respect his position demanded. Even when he'd been a boy, she had only been intent on making him strong.

And Amira... Half the time, he didn't know what to do with her. He wanted to cocoon her, wrap her in safety and only take her off the shelf when he needed her.

Loving her would make him weak, even if he knew how.

What he needed, what they both needed, was a little distance.

He was not a man who was ever going to admit that he craved a family connection. That even beneath the right he had demanded of Zufar was a desperate need for a place to belong.

"I'm a little embarrassed," Amira said instead, his sudden withdrawal clear in the tense line of her shoulders. It wasn't the complete truth, but she couldn't give him anything more knowing that he was already retreating from her.

Whatever it was he had seen in her face had utterly spoiled the post-coital haze they had been in.

"By what?" he asked, turning away from her to pull on a pair of pajamas that hung low on his sleek hips.

Fortunately, Amira didn't have to come up with a lie since a guard announced himself from outside their tent. Amira instantly pulled up the rug to cover her bare breasts.

Adir shook his head. "He wouldn't dare to come in. But it has to be important if the guard has asked Wasim for permission to disturb me. Stay in bed. And sleep a little. I will see you later."

"Later when?" she asked, the words slipping out before she could curb them.

She frowned as the guard called out again in an urgent voice.

The dialect was different but she caught the gist of it. Adir's softly spoken commands dismissed the guard, and she had no doubt that he had all but forgotten about her.

He was the sheikh now, the man who was responsible for his people.

In her hurry to get to him, she moved too fast and his arm around her waist was the only thing that stopped her from stumbling.

The impact of his hard chest against her breasts sent shock waves over her skin. Desire unfurled like petals, a sweet, slow ache in the place between her thighs.

The same desire reflected in his eyes. A wicked smile danced around his mouth. "If you want a kiss before I leave, *ya habibiti*, all you have to do is ask for it."

"I want to go."

His hands fell from her, an instant frown on his forehead. "Go where?"

"To the camp. I heard about the pregnant woman. Adir, I saw her at the henna ceremony. She didn't look good even then. I was pretty sure it is twins, but Humera wouldn't let me do a quick checkup on her."

"Humera was right to stop you. You're not their nurse. You're their sheikha."

"I will always be a nurse first, just as you'll always be a leader first. If she's suddenly bleeding, that's not good. For the babies or her."

"The mobile clinic is on its way. And Wasim will bring Humera to look after her in the meantime."

"Humera is a hundred years old and can barely stand as it is. The guard said the mobile clinic was at least five hours away at another remote village. I can be there in a half hour, I know."

"How? How do you know?"

"I know because I asked the woman which tribe she was from and then I asked Zara where they were encamped. I wanted to visit her in a few days just to make sure she was okay. I could see the desperation in her eyes."

"You haven't slept an hour all night and you weave where you stand—"

"And whose fault is it that I didn't sleep? You're the one who decided you'd avoid me for two days and then make up for it by keeping me up all night. Sex is not how we solve our arguments."

His skin stretched taut over those sharp cheekbones, his mouth a straight-pursed line. "Are you saying I kept you up against your will?"

"No. But I didn't want to deny you."

"So you only...participated? Why? Because it is your duty?"

Amira reached for him, her heart thumping against her chest. He looked so remote, so furious, and yet beneath it, it was clear that he needed her. He needed her to need him, to want him.

He couldn't bear that she might stay in this relationship for anything except that she wanted to be with him. Then why couldn't he see that she felt the same way?

That she needed to be more than just a woman carrying his child, a convenient wife, a prized asset.

She wanted to be the person he needed the most, the woman he loved beyond anyone. And anything else.

She wanted to be enough for him. This life with her—she wanted it to be enough for him.

She wasn't allowed to talk about even her feelings for him.

Why couldn't he admit that they were way past a marriage of convenience? That they belonged together—not because of the baby, but because they had chosen each other?

She wrapped her arms around him, laying her cheek on his chest. He was so essential to her and yet he didn't see that she was her own person. "Of course not. I just… It came out the wrong way. Every time we make love, I'm just as desperate as you are. Just as hungry as you are." She looked up, hoping he would see the truth in her eyes. "Adir, please let me go. I can be back by tomorrow morning."

"No. There has to be someone else." He pushed her away, none too gently, his face set in resolute lines that she hated. As if he was distancing himself from her, becoming a man she couldn't reach. "Because I know you, Amira. If I let you this time, there will be no end. Every time someone in some camp has a little ache, you'll go running. You're exhausted, you're pregnant and—"

"Why is that such a horrible situation to be in? I want to help. Even that evening, I saw a need that I could fill. Just as you have a purpose, I want to have one, too."

"Your purpose is to be my wife and the mother to our children. You will not make decisions without consulting me."

"I'm a trained nurse and to keep me locked away here when someone needs help… Don't stop me please." Not even by a flicker of an eyelid, did he relent. "I… I shall never forgive you if you take away the most important thing to me."

He stared at her, stunned, as if he couldn't quite believe her daring in threatening him. "And being a nurse is the most important thing to you?"

"Yes. It is the one thing in life that is mine, that I built, that I value," she croaked out. It was. It always had been. Until she met a stranger in the moonlight and began weaving foolish, impossible dreams. Before she forgot her own promise to herself and fell in love with him all over again.

Adir had been shaped by the harsh desert, by the finicky affections of a weak woman.

"Whether I married Zufar or some other nameless stranger my father arranged for me, whether I was resented or loved, whether I was deceived or wanted, this…this was the one thing no one could take away from me. I thought you of all men would understand how important it is to me. Strip away your leadership of these people and what remains of you, Adir? Do not do this to me."

Adir had never imagined a woman would have this much hold on him—this constant clamor to ensure her well-being and safety all the time, as he maneuvered the four-by-four over the rising and dropping desert floor to where the Peshani encampment had last been seen four days ago.

Four days ago when he had sent off his pregnant, tired and ready-to-break wife to see to another pregnant woman. For the first time in his adult life, he felt a burning resentment toward the tribespeople and their chosen mode of living.

Toward the mantle of duty that had always sat on his shoulders and yet had never felt so heavy and grasping, until today. Until now.

Ya Allah, he had barely slept and he had a hundred other matters to look to. Even this drive was unnecessary since Wasim could have easily collected her and Zara and brought them back safely.

But no, he hadn't been able to deny himself just as he hadn't been able to deny her.

With all his will, he wished he had been able to say no to her request. To tie her down in his own bed until there was no chance of her putting herself in unneeded peril.

To tell her that she had only one role to play— as his wife and as a mother to their child and as his sheikha. Only, and exactly as he dictated.

He should have held out against her demands. Even Humera, he knew, had been surprised by his assent, however grudgingly it had been given.

But one look into those wide, black eyes, the sight of the quiver of her soft mouth and the urgency, anxiety and the helpless rage that had breathed through her slender body as she had paced around him had made him relent. The way she had hugged herself, retreating from his touch, as if she meant to brace herself against the heap of hurt he would rain on her… Even the memory of how she had looked made his chest tighten as if something heavy was pressing away at him.

If he had said no, something indefinable would have been broken between them. Something he hadn't known had already breathed itself into existence.

He would have broken her. And for all his sins, Adir couldn't stand to be another man, another nameless face that controlled and molded Amira, that relentlessly beat at her spirit until it was a withered, dying thing.

He had seen it in her eyes. He would have lost something he hadn't known he had.

So he had said yes. At least, if he had been able to accompany her, it would have been better.

But the very tribal chief that had mocked Adir's parentage—or the lack of it—had sent a message. That he wanted to talk. Adir wanted dearly to punch the man in his craggy, resentful face, but he had to give the starchy, old man credit.

He hadn't liked Adir, whatever his reasons. But for the sake of his tribe, he was coming forward. He was a ruler who understood that personal matters had no weight in a leader's life.

Something Adir seemed to have forgotten in just four days.

Why hadn't the damn woman returned as

promised? Why hadn't Wasim dragged her back as he had been instructed to?

And how could he tolerate sending her away to help someone like this the next time?

He couldn't. He couldn't let her weaken him like this.

And if he didn't, she would… Would he lose her?

He could protect Amira from everything. But this urgency, this ache in his chest, what would he do if he ever lost that respect in her eyes, that affection he spied in her gaze?

And if he did somehow keep it, how long before she realized he would never love her as she deserved to be loved?

That he would always remain, at heart, a man isolated from everyone and everything.

A man who was only capable of ruling but not loving.

CHAPTER TEN

AMIRA COULD NOT believe she had succeeded in persuading Adir to let her accompany him to an oil summit he was attending in the neighboring country, the Kingdom of Zyria.

Of course, she was excited to be visiting Zyria which was a beautiful country, but it was her first official trip with Adir and she was determined to enjoy every minute of it.

Even if he had worn the most frightful scowl the whole time, from when he had arrived at the Peshani encampment to pick her up to when she had begged him to let her join him on the trip.

She had braced herself for his refusal—four days of being at the camp dealing with a difficult birth of twins without drugs or sophisticated equipment had truly tired her, a fact she was sure she wore on her face when he had arrived.

The look in his eyes when he had caught sight of her…such fury as his gaze rested on the shadows under her eyes, the sweat on her forehead since it had been her shift to watch Zareena and the babies. Amira had been terrified he would never let her attend anyone ever again in a medical capacity.

But he had ordered her into the Jeep without a word and for once, she had wisely bit her tongue and stayed silent, which she realized had gone a long way to pacify his raging temper. Not that the remoteness in his eyes had abated one bit.

Once he had agreed to let her come—a grunt from his throat while not even looking at her—he had left her to the not-so-tender mercies of Humera, who had ordered her to rest while overseeing her packing with Zara and one other woman.

Not a single word as he drove them to a private airstrip in the nearest city.

Not a single murmur in response as she had oohed and aaahed, laying it on thick, as they had embarked on the private jet that was to bring them to the capital of Zyria.

Not a single look in her direction in the three hours they had been on the flight. Though to be fair, Amira had napped for the first two, hoping that he would join her.

In the end, she had washed up, changed and joined him in the front cabin, only to be addressed oh so politely by him, told that he was tired and intended to sleep for the remnant of the flight.

Followed by quite a threat about how he would put her under house arrest for the next few months if she didn't take care to eat well and rest enough.

Having finished her salad and cheese—the only thing she could still manage to eat—Amira paved a path through the thick carpet in the main cabin before deciding she'd had enough.

If he meant to ignore her the whole week they were in Zyria, he didn't know her.

Whatever concerns he had, whatever complaints he had for her, they would have to deal with them openly. For she refused to have a silently dying marriage.

She refused to give up on this just when they were making progress.

The rear cabin was steeped in darkness when Amira entered it a few minutes later. Her breath became shallow as she let her eyes get used to the relative darkness after the blazing lights in the main cabin.

Slowly, she ventured farther in and found the bed. And on it, dressed only in sweatpants, was Adir, his eyes closed and his arm laid carelessly over his head.

What was she going to do if he was sleeping? She would surely lose her mind if she had to go another minute without talking to him. Or being away from him.

Maybe she could get into the bed and just lie close to him. Feel his heart under her palm. Soak in the warmth from his body. Just breathe him in.

She had barely undone the buttons to her jeans—they were uncomfortable enough to sit in, much less to sleep in—when he said, "I was hoping to get some rest. Alone."

She jumped back, startled. He hadn't moved a muscle nor opened his eyes. Only his arm had moved. Now it covered his eyes—a clear sign to ward her off. As if she were a pest bothering him.

She refused to be cowed. Her jeans fell off her hips and legs in a soft whisper and she stepped out of them. "I won't disturb your rest. I just…"

She shook off the sleeveless, long cardigan next, leaving the button-down shirt she had chosen for comfort.

Going to him in his bed in a shirt and bra and panties was like tweaking the tail of a tiger but she didn't care. She desperately needed to be close to him.

"You just what, Amira?" His eyes were still closed, his voice resonating in the small cabin. The husky timbre of it stretched her skin tight.

"I just need to be close to you," she said, hurrying through the words before she lost her nerve. "I know you're furious with me and yourself and you will only emerge from it when you have made some sort of decision inside that head of yours. That you will not even acknowledge me until then. But it's been a total of almost six days since you looked at me, or touched me. Or held me." She swallowed the little something that floated in her throat, determined to say her piece. "I miss you, Adir. It was bad enough that I missed you when I was with the Peshani. But to miss you when you're right in front of me is… My chest hurts."

Silence. Utter, deafening silence.

If his shock could be given form, Amira was sure it would be a giant hole in the small room, suffocating the very air out of her.

Did he still not know what was in her heart? That it was all his?

Amira had no idea how long she stood there like that, waiting for him to respond. Wretched and yet still full of hope.

"I do not like what you do to me," he began. "I... I trusted you to take care of yourself. You promised. And yet when I found you, a breeze could have blown you away. It is not just my child's well-being that concerns me. It is... You make me want to lock you up and throw away the key. To never let you out of my sight, to never again let you...attend to another woman in your life. Do not...do not push me to that, Amira."

"I did take care of myself, Adir. Please, you have to believe me. It was a difficult birth. That first night, I could not rest for fear of her life-blood slipping away while I slept. It will not be like that always."

"Always? Do you know how tempted I am to say there will never be another occasion?"

"You would not do that to me."

"I wish I could. I don't want you to look at me like you look at your father. With fear and resentment. So the only way to deal with this is to let me get control of myself. To let me treat this marriage as a polite arrangement. To let me treat you as a partner and nothing more."

"That would kill me just the same."

"To care this much for you while you demand to be true to the one important thing in your life…" such resentment filled his words that Amira gasped "…it is unacceptable."

Did he think nursing meant more to her than him? Than their marriage, than this child of theirs she carried?

"I need to learn to undo this…this hold you have on me."

Her courage faltering, Amira took one last step toward him. Without waiting for his permission, she slid into the bed and scooted close to him until their bodies were touching. Until she could breathe him in. Until the beat of his thundering heart was under her palm.

Ya Allah, she loved him so much, and it hurt to know that he would never feel even a fraction of the same for her.

Had she fallen in love with him that same evening that she had met him? To meet a man who saw her as she was, to be cherished by him—to know Adir that night had been to fall in love with him. Why else had she—who had never done anything so brave and bold in her life before—given herself to him so easily? Without a thought to the consequences when they were so horrible for her?

"What you feel, this small fear, the little bit of caring," she said, "I feel that a thousand times over. I love you so much, you own my heart. You had it from that very first time when you asked me if you could touch me. When you looked at me as if I was the most unbelievable thing you had ever seen. When you held me with such tender care that for the first time in my life, I thought, this is how I wish to be held all the time. I thought, this is how I wish to be looked at. Forever. Always. But it was a foolish dream so I grabbed the night instead with both hands.

"Do you not see, Adir? You changed everything. You changed me. You still continue to do so. For years, I lived in the fear that nothing in life would be my choice. Nursing became my identity, my reason to look forward to another day. I spoke in anger, so anxious to let you see how much I needed to help her. So worried that you will also try to mold me into what you want, not accept me for what I am.

"Continuing to be a nurse is important to me, yes, but not more than you or this baby or the family we're creating for ourselves. It is what I have wanted for so long. Somewhere to belong, someone to love with my whole heart. I would never, never put that at risk for anything."

In his silence, she saw the fear—fear for her, fear that she was beginning to mean something to him. And the need to control it. To suppress it.

Her heart seemed to hover in her throat for an eternity, her every hope thrown on a bold risk she had taken in telling him what he meant to her.

If he rejected her admission, if he so much as decided not to look at her, how would she cope?

After what felt like an eon, he turned to his side.

Heat. Hardness. Heart.

He was everything she had always dreamed of. Here in this moment with her. And yet, just a little out of reach.

His beautiful face was wreathed in shadows, hidden from her, while he studied her.

Amira closed her eyes, terrified of what she would find in his. Or what she would not find.

"I want to believe you, Amira. I have never received such a gift. I do not know what to do with it. I do not… I will never know how to return it."

And just like that, Amira's heart broke a little. But she didn't give up. She would never give up on him.

Not when she had finally understood this. Not when the man she loved was so brave, so honorable, so…full of heart, even if he denied it.

How could she love him any less even after that admission?

Her hands moved of their own accord, finding

his hot skin. The jut of his taut shoulders. His velvet rough skin. The small raspy hairs on his chest. The line of his strong throat. The bristle on his jaw. The sharp flare of his nose.

Every inch of him was so dear to her. The love she felt for him filling her with courage. To risk her heart, again and again.

"I want to be your sheikha. I already share the love you have for these fierce people, I already feel your passion for the desert that gives back so much. I would be proud to rule them by your side. I choose you, Adir. Again. This time, knowing what a..." her tears blocked her throat "...a complex, stubborn man you are. Knowing the truth of you at the core of my being.

"I choose this life with you, even knowing that it is sometimes hard and sometimes breathtakingly beautiful. All I ask is that you let me have a little of my passion, too. It is not a zero-sum game, you know that, right? Nursing gave me an identity when I had nothing else to hold onto. But now, it's tied to you, Adir, it's all you."

The silent room reverberated with her declaration. The air so heavy with tension that she wondered if she would choke.

And then he reached for her. Slowly. Softly. His breath feathering through her hair. "I missed you when you were gone. I miss you whenever you're not close to me. I wish to make you happy, Amira."

Amira caught the cry that wanted to escape her mouth. The admission seemed wrenched from him, but at least he had made it. To himself and to her. "You do. Even when you make me want to throttle you, you still make me happy."

She waited with bated breath, but he did no more than continue to stroke her cheek in a featherlight caress. Almost reverent.

He said nothing else.

How foolish she was to think he would return her grand admission. When would she realize that her husband would never be a man who admitted that he felt something for her?

Was it even his fault, when he'd been conditioned by his mother's sweetly poisoned words about what her love had done to her and to him in the process? When he saw what love was through the queen's weak mind and weaker actions?

Maybe Amira and her love would never be enough to overcome the shadow his past would always cast over his present and his future. And that was something she wanted to forget right now.

She wanted to live in this moment. The present was the only thing she would always have with him.

"Adir?"

Still another caress. Just the pads of his fingers against her chin, her nose, her eyes, her hair. Almost indifferently. As if he hadn't yet recovered from her admission.

When he ran his fingers down her neck to her breasts, the breath she had been holding rushed out of her in a painful exhale. Tears seeped to the corners, hot and scorching and it was all she could do to contain them. All she could do not to beg him to love her in return.

All of her was laid bare before him.

Did he know what a tremendous risk she had

taken? She, who had been terrified of ever finding a man who saw her, much less loved her?

When he dipped his mouth and kissed her, Amira let all the pain go. Let the taste of him wash away her doubts and fears for the moment.

When he pushed her onto her back without a word, without an acknowledgment of what she had shared, she hardened her heart.

This was all he would give. He had said it without saying it.

His desire, his respect, his loyalty...that was all she could ever have. And it was up to her to live with it.

When he ripped open the shirt and palmed her breasts with a rough urgency, she tried to convince herself that the insistent ache he created in her lower belly with such clever caresses was all she needed.

When he drove her to crazy desperation with his mouth at her breasts, she told herself that all she needed was this...this closeness with him.

When he stripped her to her skin and kissed his way down her body; when his breath fluttered over her inner thighs; when he separated her damp folds with his fingers and licked her at the spot throbbing and aching for him; when he sucked her between his lips while she writhed under his knowing touch; when she splintered into a million fragments under indescribable pleasure; when he drove into her while her muscles still contracted and released; when he came inside her with such intensity that his breath was like the bellows of a forge against her chest, Amira tried to tell herself that this was enough.

That he cared for their child was enough.

That he was trying to accept her as she was, that he was trying, despite his own instincts, not to control her was enough.

That he showed her paradise every time he touched her was enough.

She didn't need his love.

Her mind repeated the same thought in circles, round and round while she slipped into exhausted sleep.

CHAPTER ELEVEN

AMIRA HAD NEVER imagined Adir could be such a witty and fun companion as he was when they toured the capital city of Zyria in the hours he was free during the next few days.

The trip was a little surprise, he had said gruffly when she had inquired about the conference, he had planned for her since it didn't begin for three more days. Amira had thrown a pillow at him at the realization that he had always meant to bring her to Zyria with him.

For official reasons, he had said between long, languorous kisses and Amira had bit his lip then.

Of course, there had always been a devilish humor in him beneath the seriousness. But that he had let her see it, that he had dedicated so much time to spending with her, it was exhilarating and utterly joyous to be with a man who treated his wife like a queen.

No wish of hers was to be neglected.

No want of hers was to go unfulfilled.

No desire of hers was to go unmet.

She didn't remember when she could have mentioned that she had always wanted to see the campus of the famous Al-Haidar University where the first woman had trained to be a nurse almost four hundred years ago. He had had an exclusive tour arranged, with accompaniment by the current dean of the university, a strict, no-nonsense professor who very much reminded Amira of Humera.

Even more surprising was when Adir had joined her on the tour—Amira had simply assumed she would be sent off with a guard and collected in the evening while he looked into his business affairs. But he had patiently and with genuine interest sat through her lengthy interview of Mrs. Ahmed about her longstanding career.

He hadn't even frowned when Amira had admitted that she'd always wanted to finish her surgical training, too—something even Zufar couldn't have convinced her father to let her do.

When he had said maybe after the four children she wanted were in school they could talk about it, she had squealed and embarrassed him by hugging him openly in front of his aide and guard.

The next day, it had been shopping. Amira lost count of the number of dresses he had ordered for her at a couture house or the jewelry he had lavished upon her.

The next day, it was a private, enchanted dinner on the one hundred and fortieth floor of a rotating restaurant, the entirety of which had been booked just for them.

And their nights...their nights were spent in the vast luxury bed in their hotel suite overlooking the wondrous lights of the city.

In the three weeks of their marriage so far, Amira had assumed they had pushed each other to the edge of physical desire in every way. He was continuously surprised and more than overjoyed, he had said once, that she was his equal and willing partner in everything sexual.

She was mistaken.

If she had been bold before, Adir had pushed and pushed her until she was completely unashamed to parade around their hotel suite wearing nothing but her skin in front of him.

It was as if nothing could satisfy him except to experiment with debauchery in every way possible.

She hadn't even blushed when he had pushed her onto her hands and knees in front of the fireplace one evening and entered her from behind, one hand in her hair, one tweaking her clitoris, while he whispered that making love to her like that was his every fantasy come true.

How could she feel anything but glorious pleasure when he was so deeply embedded inside her that he felt as if he were a part of her?

She had only pushed back into him when he had stripped her clothes in front of the huge floor to ceiling glass windows that provided a spectacular view of the jewel of a city.

Until she was bare naked. He had cupped her sensitive breasts, driven her to the edge of orgasm with his fingers and when she had begged him to come inside her, he had taken her over the edge. The cold glass pressing into her breasts and the entire world a panorama of lights and sounds in front of her, Amira's climax had rippled through her.

If he made love to her like a man possessed, then he took such tender care of her after. In the languor that came after sex, he held her in the cocoon of his arms. They talked about their future, about the children she wanted to have, where they would live during summer and winter. He even shared his concerns about the tribes, about the political climate.

Except his past.

It stayed like an ocean-wide divide between them, somehow swallowing up every other good thing.

The days and nights he had exclusively dedicated to her—just the two of them cut off from the tribes, from the outside word—should have been paradise.

They were.

Even as the words rose to her lips again and again, Amira couldn't bring herself to say it. Already, she felt as if she had bared her soul to him. In those breathless moments, when he studied her, she knew he was waiting for her to say it again.

It was as if he was trying to lavish the world and its gifts on her, trying to make up for the one thing he could not give her.

It was not the same. Not at all.

But Amira pretended that it was. With the hope that pretending would make it feel real.

To think otherwise was to torture herself for years to come.

And as a woman who had always counted her blessings rather than drowned in her sorrows, Amira couldn't allow that.

She couldn't let her love for Adir destroy her and their marriage.

The last three days of the conference, Amira had been informed by Adir's secretary, would be the busiest. More than five nations were sitting down to discuss a treaty and oil rights, and Adir had been invited to represent the tribes.

Because of his relentless efforts to protect the tribes from each other and the encroaching governments who would see them stripped of land and settled in huts on small parcels of land they would deign to give, a seat had been created on the council for a representative of the tribes.

"Most of the deals are brokered during those casual evenings," Adir had informed her one night. Obvious pride filled his voice as he ran his fingers though her hair. "This is the first time I'm attending it with my sheikha. There will be a certain curiosity about you. Since some attending members are aware that you were…his betrothed."

Amira had frowned.

Instantly, he had kissed her temple. "I have no doubt you will be a rousing success."

Amira had waited eagerly the first evening for reports on how it had gone. Each night, there was a casual dinner set up in the reception hall where the guests and their parties were invited to mingle.

Also, because it was the first time she was meeting the world as his sheikha, for the first time in her life, she was grateful for all the hours of rigorous training in protocol and local politics she had endured from her father's aides and teachers.

Because it was going to come in handy in making Adir proud. This time, it was a role she heartily accepted, for being Adir's wife meant being his partner in everything. He had a complex mind and he readily shared his thoughts with her—whether business or politics. And that was, she realized with a quiet joy, because she had his respect.

But tonight, when the world saw her at his side, she wanted them to see her pride in her husband.

She had chosen an elegant, sea green evening gown in a light, shimmering silk that created a long, chic silhouette without overtly hugging her growing belly. Her hair she had the luxury hotel's stylist set into long silky waves, even though she knew her stubborn locks would straighten out in a matter of hours.

Since she had taken extra caution about her food and water, she had already lost the gauntness around her cheeks. She skipped the bronzer and the blush, settling for some powder and a quick swab of pink lipstick.

Her one big ornamentation was, however, the delicate diamond necklace Adir had given her just this morning.

The door to their private bedroom opened just as she had finished the last brush stroke.

Adir stood behind her, his gaze on her neck reflected in the mirror. Full of warmth and wicked humor.

Tonight, he was dressed in a simple black, three-piece suit, the white of his shirt a stark contrast to his dark olive skin.

He looked breathtaking, sophisticated, a man as easy in a suit among this crowd as he was in his robes among the tribespeople.

Even if that tribal chief had expressed doubts about Adir's parentage in the beginning, it was clear that his trust in Adir was absolute.

Whoever his father had been, whatever his blood, he was a born leader.

Why didn't Adir see that?

"You should have let me buy the other necklace."

They had argued for over twenty minutes about a necklace they had seen at a famed jeweler. Glittering and ostentatious, it had not been to Amira's taste at all.

She took his hand and kissed his palm, the aqua

scent of his cologne combined with his own making her belly clench with deep longing. "I like this one. I love that you picked this one." She met his gaze in the mirror and smiled. "It shows that you…" She let the words trail off, wary of seeing his retreat.

"What?"

"Nothing."

He pushed her carefully styled hair away from her neck and kissed her nape. His fingers lingered on her midriff. Amira's breath caught in her throat as he trailed soft kisses up her jaw and to her cheek. Yet there was nothing sexual about the kisses or the way he held her.

He didn't know his strength for his grip was tight as he clutched her to his chest. He rubbed his nose against her cheek, and pressed another kiss to his neck. "Tell me anyway."

Amira sank her fingers into his hair and arched into his embrace. "That you picked this particular piece says that you know me, Adir. It means more to me than the biggest diamond in the world."

He didn't exactly startle. But that stillness came upon him.

Amira braced herself.

With another swift kiss against her lips, he straightened and let her hair fall back into place.

Just a nod in her direction in acknowledgment of what she said.

A little smile played around his lips as she turned in his arms. "You have that glow. The one they say pregnant women have." He carefully placed his hands around her belly again, as if to measure her. "You're growing bigger."

Amira scrunched her face and hit him with her clutch.

"Hey, it is not a complaint." When she didn't quite believe him, he pulled her to him, his hands cradled at her back. "Amira…you could get as fat as you possibly could, and I would still think you beautiful."

She tucked her arm through his. "I would say the glow might be from all the orgasms you bestow."

When he laughed again, she hugged the sound

to herself. "Then I shall have to keep bestowing them. Are you ready, Sheikha?"

Amira nodded, her heart bursting to full.

The evening dinner was in the famed courtyard of the luxury hotel. Soft lavender lights illuminated lovely gardens and walkways while a buffet was laid out under a canopy.

Women glittered in long designer gowns and jewelry. While Adir introduced her to a number of people, Amira stood her ground.

More than once, she steered the conversation smoothly away from her husband's involvement in the tribes. It didn't take her more than ten minutes to realize that Adir was looked upon as a fierce, smart leader, a man who had brought warring tribes to form a cohesive faction, at least in terms of facing the neighboring nations that wanted to control them.

Since she had had a heavy snack, she mostly just tried finger food. At Adir's raised brow—the man watched her like a hawk—she sipped on fresh juice.

For almost two and a half hours, he circulated among the guests, and Amira dutifully followed him.

"You're tired," he whispered at her ear during a lull in the conversation around them. When she reluctantly nodded, he added, "Ten minutes. We will take our leave then. Although he was absent from this morning's council, I have heard that Sheikh Karim intends to show his face here. I want to make his acquaintance."

"Of Zyria?" Amira asked.

A smile of full appreciation, he nodded. "Zyria has not been a member of the council before. I have heard that Karim pushed for a seat and made it sweeter by offering to host this year's convention."

Amira nodded and surreptitiously leaned into him for support.

Not a moment later, a uniformed guard neared them. "His Highness Sheikh Karim wishes to meet you in his private office."

Adir nodded. "Tell him I will walk my wife back to our room and meet him in fifteen minutes."

More than relieved that she wouldn't have to

fake a smile anymore—for she was really tired—Amira let Adir guide her through the thinning crowd toward a different bank of lifts.

"You don't have to see me upstairs. I would rather you finish this meeting and come to bed."

She could see his reluctance, but just before he was about to speak, they turned into a vast, gleaming corridor with life-size pictures on each side. At the other end was the lift.

A dated history and timeline of grand events lined the two walls. Amira didn't even realize Adir had stilled until she swayed on her feet and realized he wasn't supporting her.

She turned and whatever she had been about to say floated away.

His skin was pale under the olive tone, a tremendous stillness in him. As if he was standing in a space separated from everything and everyone around him. The strange fear that she could never reach him again skated up and down her spine.

Heart beating a rapid tattoo, Amira studied him. "Adir?"

He didn't even stir.

Fear coating her throat, she turned toward whatever had stunned him so thoroughly.

It was a life-size picture of two men on the wall—one older and one younger, clearly father and son for anyone to see. The late King Jamil Avari of Zyria and his son, the current King Sheikh Karim.

The man Adir had been waiting to meet. Although he was a teenage boy in the picture.

But even then, the resemblance was riveting.

With a gasp, Amira looked at the next picture—this one taken recently of Sheikh Karim. She stared back at Adir and the picture, as if mesmerized.

It wasn't so much that they were alike as that they had the same bearing. The same tilt of their heads. The same arrogant nose. The same penetrating stare.

No one who would see the two men together would fail to make the connection.

The older man…he had to have been Queen Namani's illicit lover. The late King Jamil must have been Adir's father. Sheikh Karim was his half brother. Another sibling Arif didn't know.

Another chance at a family missed.

Another connection lost to him.

Had King Jamil even known that Queen Namani had given birth to his son?

What a twisted, heartbreaking tale…and in all of it, it was Adir who had suffered. Abandoned by both mother and father.

Born to a king and a queen, was it any wonder he was such a natural leader? That even as he had been orphaned and discarded to the vagaries of desert life, he had emerged as a leader who had done the unthinkable.

Amira bit back on the rage that swirled through her on his behalf.

He had been cheated of so much in life. Fear unlike she had ever known gripped her.

What would this do to Adir?

To them? To their marriage?

Panic poured through her and suddenly Amira couldn't breathe.

"Adir! Adir!"

Amira's cry roused Adir from the state of extreme shock he seemed to have fallen into. He caught her mere seconds before she would have hit the marble floor.

Her golden skin was so pale that his heart jumped into his throat. Just as before, a coldness seemed to trickle down his spine as he lifted her in his arms.

If anything happened to her because of his inattention…

He barked out an order to a nearby guard to carry a message to the waiting sheikh. Within minutes, he was laying Amira down on their bed.

But the stubborn woman refused to stay lying down. She scooted up on the bed and drank the water he brought her.

He sat on the edge of the bed, his attention split. And a deafening thunder in his ears. The last piece of the puzzle. The bastard son of a king and a queen—a dirty stain banished to the desert. Prince Zufar couldn't have known how close to the truth he was.

He should have had everything—a mother and a father and siblings—and yet he had nothing, no one to call his own growing up.

And now…now to learn that he had another

brother! A man waiting to see him a few floors down. Mere minutes away. A man who would have information about his father. Information he had wanted his entire life.

"Adir?"

The fear in Amira's voice pulled him back to the now again.

Words came and fell away to Amira's lips.

"You…do you hurt anywhere?" he asked. "I will have the doctor summoned."

Amira kept her fingers stapled over her belly, more as an anchor than any real pain. "No. I'm… fine. For a minute there, I just couldn't breathe. I…" Tears fell away onto her cheeks and she couldn't stop them this time.

She took his hand in hers, willing him to lean on her. Willing him to share the tumult she could see in his eyes. "I'm so sorry, Adir."

He ran a hand through his hair, the only sign that betrayed his inner turmoil. "So I'm not the only one who sees it? Who imagines a connection?"

"No. You…you have too many similarities to miss. You have never met him?"

"No." He pushed away from the bed, her outstretched hand left in thin air.

And just like that, Amira knew she was losing him.

"I have to go out. Will you be all right?"

"Will you confront him?"

"Yes. Maybe. I have to talk to him at the least. I owe it to myself."

"Adir, please, all you will do is bring more pain to yourself. And I couldn't bear it. I couldn't bear to see you struggle with this. Let it go, Adir. Let her go. Let the past rest. Let our future have a chance."

A growl fell from his mouth—a sound so utterly wretched that Amira's tears fell away like rivulets. Tight grooves dug near his mouth.

"I can't, Amira. I can't."

Fear gave way to fury and Amira got off the bed. "What has it brought you until now? Except diminishing the value of what you do have. Except making you wonder what could have been when you are already an honorable leader, a wonderful husband.

"Queen Namani would have done better to

leave you alone. To let you believe that you had been completely abandoned. To let you think yourself a true orphan than this...this purgatory she left you in."

"How dare you say that? She loved me. How would you feel if you were forced to give up our child?"

"I would not give up this child for anything. Do you hear me? I feel sorry for her, I do. To fall in love with a man so completely unsuitable; to have to give up the child to protect her reputation, her other children. To be filled with such resentment and poison that she hated everyone else around her... I feel pity for her.

"What I would never agree with is this... perception you have that she was a great mother. She was not. When she wrote those letters to you every year, was she truly thinking of you, Adir? When she never took a risk to see you but poured everything she felt into her letters to you? Or was it her own foolish rebellion against her circumstances? She was a weak, selfish woman."

Rage filled his eyes and yet, unlike her father,

he only seemed to retreat under it rather than lash out. "I will not hear a word against her."

"And I will not keep quiet anymore. Because I'm afraid that you will hate me for it. Because I'm afraid that you will never love me if I speak ill of her. Have you wondered why Zufar or Malak or Galila were so shocked by your appearance? So ready to reject you, resent you?

"I do not agree with what he said to you. But, Adir, she was not a good mother to any of them. Believe me, I know of Galila's childhood and her growing up. Your mother was at the very least indifferent to Zufar and Malak. But to Galila, as long as Galila was but a girl, the queen was all love and sweetness. But when Galila transformed into a beautiful young woman, a competitor to even your mother in beauty, your mother took away her love just as easily as one would remove food from a child.

"Maybe she loved you, maybe it broke her to be parted from her lover and then you. Maybe she was never right again. But when she wrote those letters to you, when she fired that resentment in you for them and fueled it all these years, stoking the fire at every opportunity, she was not thinking of you.

"She filled you with her own poison, she made you into a hard man and I hate her for it. I hate that if not for her, you would give us a chance. You would give happiness a chance."

Amira had no idea whether anything she said got through to Adir or not.

He stared at her quietly, in shock as if she had transformed into something he couldn't believe right in front of his eyes. As if she had taken a hammer and destroyed the pedestal on which his mother stood.

And Amira lost all hope.

"What will you do if Sheikh Karim refuses to acknowledge the connection between the two of you? Steal another bride? Drag his name through mud? He and Zufar are just as much innocents in this as you are."

He turned away from her and Amira had had enough.

"You have to choose, Adir."

Fury emanated in those amber eyes, turning

them to a burnished gold. "Do not dare to give me ultimatums. You're my wife."

"I'm your wife, and I love you, and I cannot bear to play second fiddle to your past. As long as you cling to the past, there's no hope. You will never see everything you already are, as I see you, as the tribes see you, as the world sees you—a magnificent ruler, a loving leader, a wonderful husband and a kind lover. You have to choose between your future and your past."

He shook his head and Amira fell to the bed, her limbs trembling.

"No. I can't. Whether I accept the past or not, I will not love you, Amira."

"That is where you're mistaken. I'm not demanding that you love me no matter what. I'm more than prepared to live with what you do give me. But I can't bear to be shuffled to second place by the past that haunts you. I can't bear to love a man whose eyes are filled with shadows of the past. To love a man whose eyes are filled with pain.

"Tell me, Adir, right this minute, can you look forward to our future, our life with this child, without forever thinking of a life you could have had? A life you should have had. With your father or your mother?"

He looked as bleak as she felt. "No."

"Then we're at an impasse. Because I will not live with a man who's stuck in some other place. With a man who's always looking back."

If she thought he felt nothing, the fury that dawned in his eyes shut down that assumption. His stillness was so unnatural given the burn in his amber eyes, the emotions rousing within.

"You have no choice, Amira. You're pregnant with my child. You're my wife. And more than anything else, you love me. You will not leave me. I admit, I'm angry right now. But when I think this through, when I'm calm once more, I will return. And our lives will resume normally."

CHAPTER TWELVE

IT WAS AMIRA'S favorite time of day when the setting sun painted the sky a myriad of pinks and oranges, and the colors were gloriously reflected in the blue waters that surrounded the palatial house.

When she walked around the beautifully manicured gardens or took the car to the evening bazaar in the nearby village to enjoy the lovely profusion of colors and smells or when she packed a small picnic and watched the sunset from the beach, she could almost forget the rest of the world.

And him.

Almost.

She could forget that her father called a hundred times a day, ready to rip her into pieces for daring to leave Adir. She could forget that when night came and she lay in that big bed in that huge bedroom, she cried herself to tears most nights. She could forget that in her waking moments, half the time she doubted herself for leaving a man who treated her with respect, kindness, even affection.

But then there were moments like this when she placed her hands on her belly, and in her heart knew that she had done the right thing.

She couldn't live with a man who didn't understand her love. Who thought it was a weakness he could use to bind her to him.

Not day in and day out, no.

Not even for her child.

She had nothing to bargain with, either. And yet instead of fear, all she felt was courage. This was what he had given her.

This courage to stand up for herself, this faith in herself and the choices she had made.

He was going to be furious with her for leaving him, but he would not force her to live with him against her wishes. She had that much faith in him. In her love.

She could not lose her self-respect just to be near him. As much as she wanted to.

* * *

She had barely put away the dishes from her dinner when she heard a car drive up the winding driveway.

Frowning, she moved to look through the kitchen window. The guard lived in the outbuilding, and the two maids that looked after the house had already retired for the night.

And then she saw him, a tall, dark form in the lights of the portico.

Her husband.

Hands and legs trembling, she made it to the living room just as he walked into the room.

Fury and something else she couldn't read settled into the lines on his face so deep he looked like he was sculpted that way. And when he opened his mouth, closed it, walked around the room like a caged wild animal and then smoothed his fingers through his hair roughly, Amira knew what the other something was.

Fear.

For her? For the baby?

"I informed Wasim where I was going before I left," she said.

The fury didn't abate at all. He stared at her as if he'd even forgotten she was there. As if the emotion was still riding him high. "You informed him?" He roared the words as if they were wrenched from him under the promise of pain.

His fingers grabbed her shoulders, biting into them. He didn't even seem to realize that he was hurting her.

Neither did she care. It was the pure torment in his eyes that swept through her. That held her transfixed.

She had never seen him so out of control. So ragged at the edge that she could almost believe he was falling apart.

"That's what you have to say about this? That you informed your guard that you're leaving me? Leaving our marriage and disappearing to God knows where? That is not how a wife behaves. Given one chance, you'll walk out on me? Is that what I should expect as a pattern for your future behavior, given the fact that you ran out on Zufar with me?"

Amira didn't even know she had swung her

arm. Not until her palm met his cheek with a re-sounding sting that sent shivers up to her elbow.

She hated violence of any sort and this was what he was reducing her to.

Tears pooled in her eyes and she brushed them away angrily. Hurt splintered through her.

"Get out. I don't want to talk to you. If this is what you think of me, there is no need for words. I want a divorce. I never…" her words came out in a broken whisper "…I never want to see you again."

And then, when she thought she would fall apart, he pulled her to him. His arms around her, his mouth pressed against her temple whispering endearments, he held her as he had done that first evening. So tenderly, so gently, as if she were the most precious thing he had ever held. As if he couldn't breathe if he let go of her.

"I hate you," she said. "I hate you for what you said, and I hate you for making me like this. I hate you for twisting my words, for hurting me. I hate you so much that I…sometimes wish I had never met you."

"No, Amira. Don't say that."

"I begged you to let me and this child be but you dragged me into your life. I begged you to stay, I laid my heart at your feet, Adir, and you trampled all over it. Still, I've stayed strong. For this child. But you…you won't let me have even this…little peace."

"I know, *ya habibi*, this is all my fault. Please, Amira, do not cry. Not over me. I couldn't bear that I hurt you. No more."

Amira stayed in that embrace, holding onto him desperately, because she knew it would be gone in a minute. If this was what he thought of her… "She's long gone, Adir. Right or wrong, she is long gone. And you can't hold onto her. And I won't blame her anymore when it is you that refuses happiness."

"I'm so sorry." His words came out broken, stuttered. "I've been out of my mind. I was lashing out, so angry with you. I'm so sorry, *ya habibiti*."

She didn't want that endearment but Amira didn't call him out for it. "I told you, I left a message and made sure you would receive it. I took your bloody plane, demanded keys of your housekeeper and moved into your house. The women here, they're loyal to you. They would have told you what I had for dinner, for God's sake, if you demanded it. I kept myself safe. I'm not a child, Adir. When will you take me seriously?"

"I was not worried about your safety. What I said, it was awful and wrong and only reflects badly on me. I couldn't believe that you could just..."

"Just what?"

"Just leave me like that. When I was desperate to believe that you loved me. Just when I was beginning to fall in love with you, too. Just when I was beginning to understand that it was already too late, that you already owned a piece of my heart."

Shock waves running through her, she stared. Stupidly.

He was apologizing and he looked even worse than when he had walked in. Clearly, what he had said to her hurt him even more than her. But now...this...

Instead of soothing her, it only made her more

mad. "Did you take anything I said seriously, ever?"

"Amira—"

She pushed away from him, wanting to look in his eyes. "You think I left just like that? You think I say words like *I love you* because I'm a naive, foolish girl? Make empty promises because I'm all fairy tales and fantasies?

"I waited all night for you to come back. I worried about what you said to Karim, I worried how he might have hurt you. You sent a message saying you were busy in the morning. You were avoiding me. I didn't do anything rash. I cried, I dried my eyes, took a shower. I even dallied over breakfast, waiting for you. And then, when you…you made it impossible for me to stay, I left. I called your pilot and arranged for him to pick me up. He couldn't even reach you. Do you know how worried I was? If I had stayed in that hotel room, I would have…fallen apart."

"You left, Amira."

He kept repeating it slowly. Amira realized he was not just angry.

And that fear she had glimpsed, it was fear that he had lost her.

Lost her forever.

The anger and hurt and fear that had been sitting like a hard lump in her chest all these days slowly began to deflate. He had been worried that he had lost her. Did she mean so much to him? Would they swing back and forth forever like this?

No.

"You declared so arrogantly that I would not think of leaving you because I loved you. Love is not a weakness, Adir. My love for you, it makes me strong."

"No, it's not a weakness, and you were right about my mother. She loved me, yes, but you were right, she was flawed, too. And in her pain, she passed it on to me. Her legacy to me became this bitterness and if not for you, I would have never seen it."

Amira thought her heart would burst out of her chest. "What do you mean?"

"I never went to see Karim that night. I stayed in the bar downstairs, just thinking, of everything you said. Such a fragile woman, such powerful words."

"I... I never want you to think I didn't understand your pain. I just... I wanted you all for myself," she said.

"No, Amira, you shone the light into a lifetime of darkness. Every word you said, as the hours passed me by, I realized all of it was right. I realized suddenly I didn't really care. There's a certain closure in learning who my father was. In knowing that he loved her just as much as she had loved him. That even though she gave me up, I was born out of love. The minute I embraced that, my desperation to see Karim fell off."

When he fell to his knees and buried his face in her belly, fresh tears pooled in her eyes.

"Everything has changed, Amira. And you're the one who has done it. All my life, I longed to be acknowledged, to be given my rightful place. I longed for a place to belong. But you are right. I already have a family. It's you and this child. It's with the tribes. There's nothing in life that I don't have. Except your love, *habibi*. You, your love, that is what completes me. I'm so sorry for hurting you. For making you feel as if you were second in my life. I love you, Amira, with everything that is in me. You're the first, Amira, in my heart. Just you."

Amira dropped to her knees and almost knocked him off his when she fell into his embrace.

She was sobbing and he was laughing, and then he kissed her. But this time, he told her how precious she was to him.

This time, there was no doubt in her mind that she had finally found a place to land.

With the man she loved.

With the man who understood her, accepted her and loved her. Just as she was.

* * * * *

LET'S TALK

Romance

For exclusive extracts, competitions and special offers, find us online:

f facebook.com/millsandboon

⊙ @millsandboonuk

🐦 @millsandboon

Or get in touch on 0844 844 1351*

For all the latest titles coming soon, visit millsandboon.co.uk/nextmonth